Teopista

A portion of book sales will be donated to the Adams Township School District Foundation's trades program. Frank and Nancy Rugani played an instrumental role in fundraising and founding this program, which provides much-needed vocational training in a growing number of fields for students in Upper Peninsula Michigan's Copper Country.

Front cover photo: Teopista Marchi Rugani in front of her boarding house in South Range, Michigan, circa 1917.

Back cover photo: Rugani's Market delivery trucks, circa 1935.

ISBN 978-1-54390-600-4

Design and layout by Chris Wisniewski of Saving Stories.
www.saving-stories.com

Teopista

a matriarch's story

based on the memoirs of Dr. Frank C. Rugani

Stephanie Nichols Boyer

For Frank and Nancy

Author's Note

Frank Rugani is a master storyteller. The son of an Italian father and a Finnish mother, Frank grew up in Michigan's Upper Peninsula in the 1940s and '50s, with no shortage of drama in the family. Frank fought his way up and out to a professional life as a dentist, and eventually came full circle, moving back home to the Copper Country in 2006. I met Frank a few years after that, when he asked me to help him write a personal memoir. As we completed work on *Teopista and Me,* named in honor of his special relationship to his Italian grandmother, he expressed a wish to tell a portion of the story in fictional form. The project turned out to be a great pleasure for me, and for Frank as well.

Most of the stories in this volume are true according to Frank's research and memory, including some of the high drama. Where facts were missing, I invented a plausible version. For example, we know that each of Teopista's first three children had a different father. Two of these men were brothers and the third was her husband. Exactly how this came to pass is lost to history, so I imagined how it could have happened. In a couple of other cases, I changed details of timing for the sake of the story. Otherwise, what follows is essentially true, hard though this may be to believe in some instances.

I am grateful to my brother, Bruce Nichols, for his insightful editing suggestions; to Paula Stahel for her encouragement and editing of an early draft; to my husband, David, for his patience as I disappeared into my study; to Chris Wisniewski for her unerring sense of design; and to Frank and Nancy Rugani for their support and enthusiasm from beginning to end.

Stephanie Nichols Boyer
Spring 2017

Two proverbs guided Teopista "Ma" Rugani's life:

"Non ti fidare di uno che non ti guarda negli occhi."
Never trust a person who doesn't look you straight in the eye.

"Si fa come si puole, non come si vuole."
We do what we must do, not what we want to do.

Loppeglia and Torcigliano Alto, Tuscany

Teopista got as comfortable as her hard-backed chair would allow, and settled one baby onto each breast. On the right was her daughter, Iolanda. On the left was her sister, Ersilia. Pista's mother was just thirty-seven years old, but with thirteen children she was pretty well worn out. Eighteen-year-old Teopista was in her prime in 1905—well endowed and lusty. Her mother needed her to serve as a wet nurse, and there was no question of saying no. Pista winced as her sore nipples again accepted two hungry mouths.

Teopista's family, the Marchis, were *contadini,* tenant farmers with no possibility of land ownership. Every member of the family worked as hard as age and strength would allow, with a large share of the farm's profits going to absentee landowners. With no running water, electricity, or money, they tended their fields, carried water, fed their large family entirely from scratch, and made their own charcoal, a process that took days and began with twigs and branches gathered in the woods. Nothing ever went to waste. When the family grew corn, they ground up the dried kernels to make polenta, burned the cobs for fuel, and slept on mattresses stuffed with the dried husks.

As a young girl, Teopista was taught to make yarn from sheep's wool, using a stick of bamboo as a hand bobbin. She was supposed to wrap the wool around the bamboo and then spin it until the wool rolled off into her fingers in strands. Older women in the village could do this lightning fast and with their eyes closed, but Pista couldn't get past the awkward stage.

She was never awkward, however, on Saturday nights, when villagers gathered to drink wine, dance, and compete to tell the best story. On these nights, Teopista pinned her thick dark hair on top of her head, put on her best dress, and hummed the whole way down the steep road from Loppeglia to the larger neighboring village of Monsagrati. Pista was a natural dancer. She swayed her hips to the music and worked the room, the boys hooting and cheering. As the energy rose, she knew just when to take it up a notch. In her signature move, she picked up a wine flask and balanced its straw base on her head as she danced. Older women looked on with a mix of admiration and jealousy, shaking their heads even as they couldn't help cracking gap-toothed smiles.

"Felice, that daughter of yours is gonna be trouble."

"*Sì*, no doubt," agreed Felice, "but what can I do?" She tapped her head. "The girl knows, up here, that she's playing with fire, but she doesn't *feel* it. In her heart, she has no idea." Felice sighed. "And she's so beautiful. Remember those days, when we were young like that?"

Pista sachayed over and gave her mother a kiss. "Mama, isn't this wonderful? I want the night to go on forever!"

"I love you, *cara*," said Felice. "Just be careful with those boys, okay?"

"Sure, Mama, don't worry."

Teopista understood her mother's warning, but dancing her heart out on those Saturday nights, she felt happier than at any other time in her life. She couldn't get enough of the feeling of holding the crowd in thrall, the boys and men especially. Over time there was one young man who began to invade her thoughts, not just at the dances but also during the week, as she scrubbed floors and performed her farm chores. Faustino Pini lived two houses down. Their families had been friends for generations, and Faustino was handsome and macho. He clearly desired her, and Teopista began to lie awake in her bed at night, long after the rest of the household had fallen asleep, her stomach flipping over at the thought of him.

One Saturday night, after a highly charged dance with the bottle on her head, Pista took a tumbler of wine and stepped outside for air. Moments later Faustino appeared, acting casual.

"Hey Pista, nice dancing in there."

It was a moment she had imagined many times. *"Grazie, Faustino."* There was a pause. "Beautiful night, isn't it?"

"Sì, molto bello." He leaned in. "But not as beautiful as you."

Her cheeks flushed.

"Put down your glass, Pista, and let me kiss you! I've waited a long time for this."

She looked around to be sure her mother wasn't watching, and allowed Faustino one kiss. With her lips on fire and her stomach doing a double flip, she pushed him away. "That's all, Faustino. Mama will kill me."

"Okay, Pista, but I'll be back. I want you so bad." He leered at her.

There was no possibility of sleeping that night. The cornhusks in the mattress she shared with her sister Corradina made noise every time she moved, so she willed herself not to toss and turn. She could not wait to see Faustino again.

The tiny village of Loppeglia, tucked into the Tuscan hills above Lucca, was made up of twenty families who lived in narrow stone houses, built into the hills and crammed with people—children, parents, grandparents, and any other relatives who might need a place to lay their heads at night. Surrounding the homes were rings of terraced soil, planted with olive trees and grape vines. The fortunes of the *contadini* rose and fell with the growing conditions for these fruits, but never rose very far. Landowners did none of the work and took the majority of the money, while the *contadini* subsisted on a small share of the harvest.

Each autumn, on the day the farm manager determined that the green olives were just ripe enough, children skipped school and the village came out to harvest. Men climbed ladders to rake the trees and pick fruit by hand, while women and children gathered whatever dropped to the ground. To preserve the unsurpassed quality of the first press, bruised olives were set apart for a secondary pressing.

Over the years, the farm's trees had been carefully pruned to maximize production, using a method handed down over

3

generations. A good olive tree was hollow in the middle and cup-shaped, with spiky branches at the rim of the cup. Teopista loved the local proverb about these trees: *Agli olivi, un pazzo sopra e un savio sotto.* "A mad man at the top of the olive tree, and a wise one at the roots."

To occupy her mind during long hours of bending to pick up olives, she thought about which villager was the mad man and which the wise one. There were several candidates for the mad man, maybe because the same few families had farmed these hills for generations. This year she chose Luigi, who stalked up and down the streets of the village, shaking a stick and muttering. Pista wondered whether Luigi had been born mad, or whether something made him that way. Had someone wronged him? Had he experienced a trauma? She was old enough to know that people could be awful to one another, but no one had told her anything about Luigi. Bending down to gather green fruit all day, Teopista passed the time by inventing stories in her mind and wondering about her chosen mad man. And then she thought about Faustino, and her stomach flipped all over again.

When the harvest was complete, time was of the essence. Olives had to be pressed quickly before they spoiled and fermented, so the communal *frantoio*—the press—in the nearby village of San Martino in Freddana was entered into full-time service. The *frantoio* was nearly as sacred as the local church. In an honest moment, a villager would say it was the more important of the two. The building contained a huge stone basin, kept perfectly clean, with a five-foot millstone that circled the basin when pulled by an ox. Oxen had to be specially trained to do this tedious work. In San Martino, it was Paolo Ricci who had a special touch with the massive beasts. Paolo understood how to entice them to perform the tedious task of walking in slow circles for hours on end, rewarded by the nosebag he kept stocked as they trudged.

At pressing time, the contadini dumped sack after sack of olives into the basin, to be mashed by the millstone into a thick, greenish pulp. When the chief oil-maker determined that the mash was of just the right consistency, workers transferred it to a press where the men themselves took on the role of oxen, leaning their full weight onto a handle that lowered a huge block of wood onto the mash. The extract from this first pressing became the very best oil, whisked away by the landowner for sale at premium prices. The remaining mash was mixed with lower-quality bruised fruit for a second round. This oil was not valued by the landowner, so he let the farmers' families keep it.

On one special night of the year, *contadini* got to enjoy the very best of the first pressing. When the intense work of harvesting and production was finally done, people from all nearby villages gathered to celebrate. Fatigue dropped away as they sang, danced, and ate crostini dipped in fresh, peppery oil. Nothing tasted as good as this oil they had painstakingly created themselves.

The harvest celebration was famous, and infamous, as a night for lovers. Teopista would never forget the celebration of November 1905. She was seventeen years old and on top of the world. She danced her heart out at the party, drank wine, and tasted the best olive oil ever made. She felt Faustino's eyes on her all night, and finally he approached. "Come walk with me, Pista."

She knew her mother was watching but, flushed with wine and excitement, she didn't care. She stepped out with her man and they headed up the hill toward Loppeglia, to a favorite lookout spot. There was a chill in the night air. Faustino put his arm around her and drew her close as they sat on a stone wall. After a few minutes like this, Teopista sensed that Faustino was nervous.

"Pista," he said finally, "I have something to ask you."

"Sure, Faustino, what is it?"

"I . . . I . . . Pista . . . Marry me!" he blurted out. "I think of you day and night. Please, make me the happiest man alive, and marry me!"

Pista caught her breath. Every cell in her body wanted this man, and he wanted her back. It was a dream. A small voice in

5

the back of her mind urged caution, but she felt light-headed and overwhelmed with emotion.

"Faustino! *Sì,* yes, I will marry you! Yes!"

Grazie a Dio! His eyes shone, and he jumped up and turned toward the valley. "We're going to get married!" he shouted out to no one in particular. They laughed, and kissed. "I am the luckiest man in all Italy!"

They ran back down the hill, where Teopista found her mother at the party. "Mama, we're getting married!"

Felice regarded her exuberant daughter. "Congratulations, *cara.* I'm happy for you." She touched her daughter on the shoulder. "Are you sure, my dear, that he is the right one? That you are ready for a new life?"

"Yes, Mama, I am sure. I've known Faustino forever. He is handsome and a hard worker and he adores me. And don't worry, Mama, I will help with the farm just as I always have. Mama, I am so happy!"

Felice didn't try to advise her dreamy daughter in that moment. Let Pista have her bliss while she could.

A month later, all of Loppeglia turned out for the wedding of Faustino Pini and Teopista Marchi. Young children, including all eleven of Pista's sisters and brothers, put on their Sunday clothes and bounced around the church. Mothers smiled wistfully. Fathers ogled the beautiful bride, while a dozen young men swallowed their jealousy. Damn that Faustino! He had beaten them to the seductive dancer with a big laugh and curvy hips, the one strong enough to carry water and perform farm chores without complaint. Every available man in the region wanted Pista, and now she was taken. The defeated rivals shook Faustino's hand and mumbled congratulations, but at the wedding reception they drank too much and cried into their grappa.

Teopista began her married life by moving in with her in-laws. Her own home was stuffed beyond capacity, while the Pinis were able to clear a room for the newlyweds to share. Faustino's parents were kind. They were proud that their son had made such a good marriage, and they welcomed Teopista's help at home. Even with this warm welcome, it was a good thing that Pista was so happy with Faustino, because she found herself working harder than ever. Each morning, after helping her mother-in-law clean the house and bake bread, she would go two doors down to her own mother's home and perform the same chores there.

Two months after her marriage, Pista began to wake up feeling funny. It wasn't serious, but she wasn't herself. The *contadini* were raised with the understanding that they couldn't afford to indulge minor illnesses, and Teopista was never a complainer, so she ignored the discomfort and carried on without telling anyone. At night, though, she was so tired she could barely keep her eyes open. When Faustino tickled and teased her at bedtime, a game she had initially found thrilling, she grew unable to laugh and reciprocate. One night, in utter exhaustion, she turned toward the wall, and a side of Faustino emerged that she hadn't seen before. "Pista," he hissed. "What's wrong with you? You will please me when I want you!"

"I'm sorry, Faustino." She tried to appease him. "I'm just so tired. I can't keep my eyes open. Tomorrow, okay, *amore mio?*"

Faustino turned away from her, and neither of them slept very well, despite their fatigue.

A month later, Teopista was scrubbing the floor for her mother-in-law when she sat up with a start. Her monthly visitor—where was it? Was it possible . . . Yes, it must be. She dropped her scrub brush and ran over to her mother's house. "Mama, I think I'm pregnant!" She recounted her symptoms as Felice nodded her head.

"Sit down, *cara*," she told her daughter. "This is wonderful news, but it will change your life forever." Felice then confided in Pista that she herself was also pregnant, with her thirteenth child. Mother and daughter would experience pregnancy together, and a child and a grandchild would be born at nearly the same time.

For his part, Faustino was overjoyed. "*Amore*, a baby! I will be a father!"

Things were a little better at night after that. Faustino kissed his wife's belly and held her more gently. He was kinder when she said she was too tired for love. But Pista didn't forget the anger she'd seen. Her handsome, exuberant husband had a mean streak.

Teopista had absorbed a lot of knowledge of pregnancy and childbirth by observing her mother over the years. She was not surprised when she felt sick in the mornings, nor when the sickness passed. Eventually she grew so large and awkward that labor couldn't come soon enough. The day her water broke and the tension of waiting was finally over, she closed her eyes and took a breath. Childbirth was risky in those days, but Teopista was strong and she held her mother's image in her mind. If Felice, who was not half as robust as her daughter, could do this many times over, surely Pista could do it once. Assisted by the village midwife, she labored all night before giving birth to a daughter. They named her Iolanda, after Faustino's mother. Holding her tiny baby on her chest, Teopista beamed. "Look at her! She is perfect."

Two weeks later, Felice herself felt her water break. After so many births, her labor lasted about twenty minutes, and out popped baby Ersilia. "My darling," she said to her ninth daughter, "you, too, are magnificent. And now maybe the Lord will agree I have enough children." Felice was so tired, and she had almost no milk to offer.

The next morning, when Teopista came over to meet her new sister and to nurse Iolanda, Felice moved slowly to a nearby chair, with Ersilia cradled in her arms.

"Pista, I have something important to ask you. Please listen before you reply. I am worn out and dry, as you see. I need your help. I must ask you to nurse your sister Ersilia so she will grow strong and healthy. You are sitting and nursing anyway, and if you do this, I will have time to care for the family and the house." Teopista opened her eyes wide. It was hard to view her mother as either old or dry, but when she really paid attention, she could see Felice's deep fatigue.

"Well yes, of course, Mama. I will do this." And so she settled Iolanda onto her right breast and Ersilia onto her left, for the first of what would be hundreds of times.

That night, Faustino came home at the end of a long day tending the vineyards. He kissed his wife and his baby daughter, and the Pini family sat down to supper.

"Faustino," Teopista waited until her husband had had a glass of wine and something to eat before breaking the news. She knew he would not be happy about the nursing arrangement. "I have something to tell you."

As he absorbed the idea that his wife would be nursing her sister at the same time as his daughter, Faustino's face grew taut. Pista knew he would not yell or throw anything in the presence of his family, and he did not. He said nothing.

Later on, when the two were alone in their room, with Iolanda asleep on her small mattress, Faustino had calmed down a little but was still unhappy. "Pista, I don't like this. Your sister will get half of our daughter's milk. Our baby will be weak, just because you couldn't say no to your mother. It's not right."

As overjoyed as Faustino was at the birth of his daughter, he had also felt his wife's affections shift away from him and toward the baby. She was over at her mother's house even more than before, and with this nursing arrangement, she would practically live over there. Faustino was too proud to admit it, but he felt neglected.

Teopista had prepared for this conversation, and she had not lost the wit and charm that softened up the most macho of men. She knew what to say.

"Faustino, *amore mio,* do not worry. Be proud that your wife has plenty of milk to feed two strong, healthy babies. Not everyone can do this, you know. You and I, we are blessed. Mama knew you would support me, because you are a good and strong man." Pista went on flattering her volatile husband until his mood lifted.

"Okay, Pista. You have my permission. But—don't forget who comes first." He pulled her down onto the bed in a tight embrace, kissing his wife's pillowy breasts and her belly still soft from pregnancy. She laughed and returned his embrace.

Faustino accepted the rapid changes in his household, and he still adored his wife, but he began to spend more evenings out with the village men, drinking wine and exchanging news that filtered through from other parts of the country. In 1906, a new topic was generating heated discussion: the possibility of going to America. After Italian unification in 1871, a wave of emigration to North America had begun in the south and had grown steadily. Millions of men had made the decision to go, and word came back that southerners were making enough money in America to return to Italy and buy their own land.

"Maybe we should try it," the more restless Tuscan men began to say. After a few glasses of wine, they got cocky. "In America there are jobs. We can go there, work for a year, and come back rich!" Gino Corsi shook his head. "If the boat over there doesn't kill you, something else will. The whole thing is a scam. I'm not having any of it." Others were ready to dream. Francesco Rugani, from the neighboring village of Torcigliano Alto, was taken with the idea—and so was Faustino Pini. If he came back with money, Faustino knew, he could buy his own farm and never work for someone else again. He could do right by his wife and daughter, and take his place as a landowner.

Iolanda was still an infant when Faustino approached his wife with determination one evening. "Pista, come take a walk with me. I have something to tell you."

Teopista had a feeling she knew what he was going to say. Talk of America had spread throughout the village, and she knew her husband. Not only would he want to go, he would want to be the first in the village. She was right. When he told her he had decided to go to a place called Baltic, Michigan, where he would make a lot of money as a miner and come back rich, she was prepared. *"Amore,"* she said, "I will miss you, but you do as you must."

What she did not say was that a small part of her was relieved. Faustino was not the easiest husband, and truthfully, she missed her old life as a free-spirited young woman. She had her baby, of course, and her responsibility to her tiny sister, but life would be a little simpler with Faustino in America.

She revealed these thoughts to no one, and her tears were genuine as she said goodbye to her husband on the day he departed. "Be careful, Faustino, and journey safely." The week-long crossing of the Atlantic in the steerage section below decks was well known to be miserable. People often became ill, and some never made it to Ellis Island.

Faustino Pini's departure was the talk of Loppeglia, and quickly filtered down to the weekly gatherings in Monsagrati. As time passed, no one knew how Pini was actually doing in America, but the more the men discussed it, the more convinced they became that he must be getting rich. Francesco Rugani was particularly agitated. "That *bastardo*. First he marries Pista, and now he is beating us again." Francesco became consumed with thoughts of showing up Faustino Pini, and within a few months he declared that he, too, would go to Baltic, Michigan, and get rich.

On the Saturday night before Francesco's departure, the villagers gathered for a bittersweet party. Teopista danced her heart out, even taking Francesco's hand and pulling him out on the floor to dance with her. "Cecco, please send news from America of how you are doing, and tell us about Faustino, too," she told him. She had heard nothing from her husband in five long months.

One evening, after Francesco Rugani set sail, a young man appeared at the Marchis' door in Loppeglia. It was Giuseppe Rugani, Francesco's older brother, who had walked more than three hilly hours from Torcigliano Alto to see them. Teopista had moved back in with her mother and her huge family after Faustino left. They loved each other dearly, but the Marchi home was impossibly crowded.

"Giuseppe!" Teopista's surprised parents offered him a grappa from their small store. Beppe, as he was called, was known to be a good man, keeping his responsibility to his parents as the oldest son, but why had he walked all this way? They sat together sipping their drinks, and soon Beppe revealed his purpose. "I have something to ask you and Teopista," he said to the elder Marchis. "My family wonders if you would consider allowing Pista to come live at our house, to help our mother. Mama is overburdened caring for the house and family, and she has become unwell. There aren't enough girls in our home, and the men are working extra hours to make up for Cecco's absence. We could offer Pista and Iolanda their own room, and we would treat them as our own."

Felice and Adolfo exchanged a glance. It was true that they had more children than they had space. Giuseppe came from an honorable family, and his mother needed the help.

"Pista," said her father, "what do you think of this idea? It is okay with us if you are willing."

Teopista tried not to look overly happy. In truth it had been hard for her to return to her family home. The younger children pulled on her skirts all day, and she was tired of the same old chores. Even those same tasks in a different house would feel better. Plus, she couldn't deny the appeal of Giuseppe Rugani. He and his brother Francesco had lavished her with attention on Saturday nights in Monsagrati, and it wouldn't be so bad to have someone new to talk with in the evenings. "Yes, Papà, I am willing."

Within the week, Teopista and Iolanda made the move from Loppeglia to Torcigliano Alto, and Pista brought gusto to her role in the Rugani household. She could get Giuseppe's mother, Rosa, to laugh, which no one else could do, and she had the whole family rolling on the floor with her imitations of local characters.

At night, after Iolanda and the younger children had been put to bed, Teopista and Giuseppe sat at the table and talked. Beppe knew how to listen, a quality uncommon among the local men. One evening, after a couple of glasses of wine, Pista found herself telling Beppe about Faustino. She loved her husband's enthusiasm and his good looks, but not the temper he had revealed after they were married. No sooner were the words out of her mouth, than she felt disloyal. It was not right to complain about her husband to another man, and she resolved not to do it again. But Faustino had been gone for many months. Pista's new life was satisfying, and, in her honest moments, she realized she did not miss him very much. His presence was gradually fading, like paint on a sun-drenched wall.

Early in 1907, a letter came from Francesco. He had a job, he wrote, as a trammer in a copper mine in Baltic, Michigan. He lived in a boarding house with ten other men, where he received plenty of good food. However, it was going to take some time to earn enough money to buy the land he and Giuseppe dreamed of. "Beppe, I am writing to ask if you will come join me. Together, we could save money twice as fast. There is plenty of work here, and I miss you. Please come to America."

This letter rocked the Rugani household. Teopista listened as Rosa and her husband, Dionisio, along with Beppe and the next older sons, spent hours discussing Cecco's request. Could they manage without both Giuseppe and Francesco? The third and fourth sons straightened their shoulders. "Yes, Papà, we can do it." It would mean more work for the teenagers, but their status in the family would rise. They were tired of being overlooked, and this was an opportunity. "Not that we wouldn't miss you, Beppe!" They elbowed their brother and laughed.

But did Beppe want to go? He looked down at the table for a long moment, and then turned to his parents. "I want both things. I want to be here with you, working on the farm and supporting our family, and I want to go to America and make money with Cecco, so we can come back and buy land of our own and make a better life. Let me think about it."

Teopista lay awake that night with the terrible realization that she did not want Beppe to go. It struck her that she had fallen a little bit in love with him, despite being married to Faustino. She had not acted on her feelings, nor had Beppe ever touched her, but there was an undeniable energy in their night-time conversations. She would keep these feelings secret, but she found herself praying that he would not go to America.

Two days later, the family gathered again with great anticipation. Beppe had reached a decision: he would go make money in the mines with Francesco. "Just for one year," he told them. "Then we will come back and buy land. The sacrifice will be worth it for the family."

Saying farewell yet again to a young local man headed to

America, Teopista fought back tears. She knew that without Beppe or Francesco, life at the Rugani home would dull to gray. She was not yet twenty years old, but Pista felt the front edge of despair. Was she destined to a life of repetitive domestic labor? What if Faustino, Francesco, and Giuseppe never returned? They said it would only be for a year, but anything could happen. Maybe they'd fall in love with American girls and decide to stay there. Pista walked slowly back to the Rugani house and took a deep breath.

"Hi, sweetie." She manufactured a smile for her young daughter and lifted her into her arms. "It's you and me, sunshine, and I love you so much." Iolanda wrapped her small arms around her mother's neck, and Pista resolved to remember what mattered most. She had a beautiful child, devoted parents, and a good adopted family in the Ruganis. The air smelled of olive trees and rosemary, and it was a sunny day in Torcigliano Alto. Pista scooped out flour for the day's baking, and got back to work.

The Rugani household established a new normal, with the younger brothers stepping up to prove they could fill the shoes of their elders now in America. Teopista performed her chores with as much cheer as she could muster, and after a few weeks began again to entertain her family and make Rosa Rugani laugh. She no longer danced with the wine bottle on her head, but she did bring her expansive personality to the Saturday night gatherings in Monsagrati, where she got to visit with her parents and catch up on news of Loppeglia.

Months passed, until one day in 1908, a letter arrived. Teopista ran to tell the family. "Rosa! It's a letter from Beppe and Cecco!" They ripped open the letter and found news they'd been hoping for. The brothers were coming home. Villagers buzzed with speculation. "They have become rich, and the Ruganis will have their own farm!" "Nah, they're coming home because it was all a big lie. Poor Italians cannot go to America and suddenly grow rich. It's impossible."

Teopista and the Rugani family wondered these things, too, but mostly they just couldn't wait to see their men. Even the younger brothers were excited. They had discovered how much work fell to the oldest boys at home, and were no longer so sure that the accompanying higher status was worth it. As for Pista, she found herself putting the wine bottle back on her head and moving her hips on Saturday night.

It felt like an eternity, but was only about three weeks between the arrival of the letter and the return of Beppe and Cecco. When the day finally came, the whole village rushed out to greet them, cheering and laughing and peppering them with questions. What's it like over there? How was the work? Are you rich?? Giuseppe and Francesco broke down in tears, kissed the ground, and put off all questions until the evening. They wanted to talk with their family first.

Around the Rugani table, stories began to come out. The eight-day trip across the ocean was as difficult as everyone had said it would be. The steerage compartment, on the bottom deck next to the steamship's engines, was loud, crowded, and dirty, and it stank. Two hundred people were packed into one compartment. Each passenger was assigned a metal berth and given a mattress stuffed with seaweed. They each got a life pre-server that doubled as a pillow, and a tin pail and utensils for meals that were served out of a huge tank.

"The food was so terrible that I didn't care how little we got," said Giuseppe. "I lost five kilos on that ship. Even worse, when people became ill, there was no way to get away from them."

"*Sì,*" said Francesco. "And the ocean is so rough that when you climb up for air, the ship rocks up and down and nearly knocks you over. It's like this!" He demonstrated trying to stand upright on a moving ship, and everyone laughed.

As the first to travel, Francesco had had no idea how to get to Baltic, Michigan. When he quizzed the other passengers on his ship, none of them had heard of it, which was disconcerting. They did offer some advice: "When you get to Ellis Island, write the name of the place on a paper and pin it to your coat."

So that's what Cecco did. Wearing his "Baltic, Michigan," tag, he slowly passed through all the lines and the physical exams at Ellis Island. When he emerged without restrictions, a man with a handlebar moustache and false smile beckoned him to the currency exchange counter. The Ellis Island exchange was notorious for taking advantage of bewildered immigrants. The man took Francesco's pile of scraped-together *lire* and handed him twenty-five dollars. With no way of knowing whether or not the exchange was fair, Cecco took the money. Then he pointed to the "Baltic, Michigan," note on his lapel, and was directed to a staircase that led to a railway station. There, finally, a stranger in America was kind to the confused traveler. A social worker helped Francesco buy a ticket to Chicago, and handed him a card that read, *"To the Conductor, Please show the bearer where to change trains, as he does not speak English."*

The train to Chicago took all night. Francesco was exhausted but on edge. With no idea where Chicago was, he did not know whether to expect a trip of two hours or twenty. He couldn't read the words on the card he carried and didn't know whether anyone would help him, so he sat wide awake all night. America must be an impossibly huge country, he thought. How could the train run for so long and still not reach Chicago? He was relieved the next morning when a conductor came through the car, calling out something that sounded like "Chicago." Weary passengers gathered their bags, and the conductor motioned to Cecco to do the same.

At the door of the train, the conductor pointed Francesco in the direction of an agent who sold him another ticket. Again he did not know how much it should cost or how far he had to go. He would not sleep until he had reached this mysterious "Baltic" on which he had pinned all his hopes. It was a good thing Cecco did not allow himself to nod off, as there were two more train changes before he boarded the Copper Range Railroad car that would finally take him to Baltic.

The family in Torcigliano Alto listened wide-eyed as Francesco recounted his story of arrival in America. Somehow this son of a tenant farmer, who spoke no English and had never ventured farther than a few kilometers in his life, had traveled across the ocean and found his way across an enormous strange land. Francesco told his story with spirit and humor, enjoying how closely everyone listened, including the beautiful Pista, who hung on every word.

From the moment Francesco stepped off the train in Baltic, the Copper Range Company was in charge. Immigrant men did not travel to Michigan's remote Copper Country unless they hoped to find work, and the Copper Range mining company needed them all. Cecco was taken to a boarding house, fed a hearty meal, and shown to a bed, onto which he collapsed and slept for twelve hours. When he awoke he was fed again, and handed a tin bucket containing his next meal. There was no need to go looking for a job; a fellow boarder motioned to Francesco to come with him, and showed him where new men gathered to begin work at the copper mine.

Francesco was assigned to the job of trammer, the lowest rung on the ladder. *"Dio mio!"* he told the family. "That first day, I thought I was going to die." It was a trammer's job to ride deep underground into the mine, load tons of copper ore onto large wheeled carts, and then use brute force to push the carts to a location in the shaft where they would be lifted to the surface. Francesco illustrated his story by showing how, at the end of his first twelve-hour shift, he was so sore he could hardly lift his arm high enough to drink a glass of wine.

At the end of a six-day week, he received the first paycheck of his life: eleven dollars and twenty-five cents. He didn't yet understand the value of an American dollar, nor did he realize how much of his small pay would be taken by room and board and company deductions. All he knew was that he had a job in America. "I got paid real money! I was making it in America."

As weeks passed, Francesco's body adapted to the demands of the job. Along with rock-hard muscles, he developed an understanding of the social networks and hierarchy of the mining life. The Italians in Baltic naturally gravitated to each other, as did ethnic groups from all over Europe and Russia who had made their way to the same obscure location in America's Upper Midwest. From his countrymen, Francesco learned that his trammer's job was the lowest paying in the mine. The best jobs were only available to Cornish workers, who spoke English and had been in America longer. Italians were only going to get so far.

Even so, most men he met were grateful for the work. Like Cecco, they dreamed of becoming landowners back home, and the only way to do so was to earn money in America. Mining jobs were plentiful, so they put up with the low wages, the dangers of working underground, and the indignity of being treated as second-class citizens.

As Francesco's understanding grew, he realized that he and Beppe would never have enough money to buy land unless they both had jobs, and so he had written the letter asking his brother to join him.

Now Beppe picked up the story. "That trip across the ocean! I would rather take the place of an ox in the *frantoio* all day long than lie there like a cow in the stinking steerage copartment." But the rest of the trip, from New York to Michigan, was not so bad. Cecco had told his brother what to expect, so Beppe knew he could fall asleep on the train to Chicago. Francesco got his brother a place in the same boarding house, showed him where to go on his first day of work, and introduced him to the Italians he'd met. In a very short time, Beppe had grown the same massive muscles as his brother, and together they earned twice as much money. Four dollars a day.

From here, the brothers' story grew more subdued. Upon re-entering Italy, they had converted their savings into *lire,* which they now laid out on the table in a pile. It was more money than the family had ever seen in one place, but it was only enough to purchase a very small piece of land, nowhere near enough to support the family.

Everyone let this reality sink in. "My sons," said Rosa, "what matters is that you have come home, where you belong. *La famiglia* is together again. Stay. Forget about that pipe dream of America."

Beppe and Cecco had no intention of turning around and boarding another steamship anyway. They were unlikely to forget about America, but for now it was irresistible to be back in Torcigliano, eating their mama's cooking and working above ground, outside in the Tuscan sunshine.

For Teopista, life catapulted into full color. There were now two lively brothers in the house, bringing jokes and stories, and, yes, paying her the kind of attention she had been missing for many months. She delighted in the way Beppe and Francesco competed to tell her the best story or elicit the biggest laugh. The Rugani household was full of energy, and Pista hummed through her daily tasks.

One afternoon Giuseppe was out pruning olive trees when Francesco found Teopista in the garden. "Pista, it's a beautiful day. Let's take a walk together, just for a little while." Iolanda was being cared for by the Rugani daughters, who adored her, and it wasn't yet time to cook supper, so Pista agreed. An undeniable energy had been building between her and Cecco, and his invitation gave her a little thrill.

They headed up a steep path to a secluded terrace, out of sight and sound of the house and the laboring men. Pista's stomach was flipping over, just as in the old days with Faustino. She was still a young woman in her prime, and her husband had been gone so long she barely remembered what he looked like.

Cecco turned to her and whispered words that made her light-headed: "Pista, I think of you all the time. You are the most beautiful, desirable woman I've ever known." She did not resist as he pulled her in for a kiss. Within minutes Teopista and Cecco were on the ground under cover of the trees, releasing their pent-up desire.

That evening it was all they could do to keep their emotions in check, and over the coming days the two found repeated ways to meet on the secluded terrace. They would wander away separately, to keep from arousing suspicion, and after a rendezvous, Francesco would join the men at work while Teopista returned to her duties at home.

One day Dionisio needed someone to make a trip to Lucca, the region's commercial center. Pista had an idea. "Cecco! I don't ever want to forget these wonderful days! Let's go to Lucca for your father and have our photographs taken while we're there. I will put them in a locket so I may always carry you next to my heart." The Ruganis preferred to dress well when they went to town, so it was not surprising when Pista and Cecco put on their Sunday clothes for the outing. No one commented that Pista had paid extra attention to her hair, and off they went, down the long winding road. In the studio of photographer Arcangelo Miniati, they were a little nervous as each posed for a formal portrait. They dared not take a photograph together, but they emerged with two tiny images, which Teopista placed in a locket and hung around her neck. Cecco inserted a photo of Teopista into his watch fob.

In the summer of 1908, after a few weeks of the clandestine meetings with Cecco, Pista felt a familiar mild nausea in the morning. *"Caro,"* she said, as they lay under their favorite olive tree, "Are you ready for some news? I'm quite sure I am pregnant."

Francesco sat up. *"Amore!* How wonderful! We will have the most beautiful child on earth."

"But," he said after a moment, "we will have to tell them."

Teopista had already thought of this. *"Sì, amore mio,* we will have to tell the family."

They weren't sure whether to be more worried about Rosa and Dionisio, who would be upset that Teopista had betrayed her husband while living under their roof, or about Giuseppe, who would likely be jealous. They agreed to put off the difficult conversation until the last possible moment, when Teopista had grown too large to disguise her condition any longer.

Pista was a curvy farm girl, so they were able to keep their secret longer than some women might, but as she began to outgrow her skirts, Pista knew it was time. She and Cecco waited until Iolanda and the younger Ruganis had gone to bed one evening, and then asked Rosa, Dionisio, and Beppe to sit with them at the table where so many significant conversations had been held.

Cecco was nervous. "Mama, Papa, Beppe." He paused. "We have to tell you—I don't know how to say it—well, I'll just tell you. Pista is pregnant!" They cringed and waited for the reactions.

Rosa regarded them. "I am not surprised," she said. "It's been perfectly obvious that the two of you were sneaking off. I feared it might come to this." Pista and Cecco could not hold her gaze. She knew! Pista was mortified. "Rosa, I am sorry. The last thing I wanted to do was cause you pain." She started to cry.

Beppe wasn't surprised, either. "Cecco, I've seen the way you are with Pista, but I didn't want to believe it. How could you?" Francesco looked down at the table.

Dionisio was the only one who seemed caught off guard, and he was furious. "Francesco!" He pounded the table. "You have brought shame upon our family! The Marchis trusted us with their daughter—their *married* daughter—under our roof, and what do you do?! You are absolutely stupid!" He did not want to yell at Teopista, so he didn't even look at her.

The Ruganis got angry in the classic Italian style. They blew up, stayed angry for a while, and then made up and carried on. Dionisio and Rosa were composed when they summoned Francesco and Teopista to the table two days later. "All right. You know the saying, *Si fa come si puole, non come si vuole.* 'We do what we must do and not what we want to do.' Here's what you must do. This baby will take the surname of Pini. You, Teopista, will write your husband a letter and ask him to come home. Tell him you miss him, and do not under any circumstances tell him about this baby. When the baby is born, you will raise the child as if it were born to you and your husband, and when your husband returns, you and he and your children will live together in the proper way. Meanwhile, there will be no more foolishness between the two of you. Is that understood?"

Pista and Cecco nodded miserably. Dionisio was right, they knew, but his words made them want each other even more. They said goodnight with heavy hearts, Pista fingering her locket and trying to keep her sobs quiet, so the family would not hear.

In March 1909, Teopista Marchi gave birth to a son, Giuseppe Vincenzo Pini. She and Francesco chose the name "Giuseppe" to honor Beppe Rugani, whom they both loved dearly. It went unspoken that they felt guilty for having met behind his back.

In truth, Teopista felt worse about hurting Beppe than she did about Faustino Pini, the man she had married so impulsively more than three years before.

Married she was, however, and as Dionisio instructed, Teopista wrote to her husband, not mentioning the pregnancy but asking him to come home. Lacking an address, she simply wrote in care of the Copper Range Company in Baltic, Michigan, and wondered if he would receive her letter. A month later came a reply. Yes, he would come home, but it might take a while. Work was going well and he wanted to earn more money before returning to Loppeglia, at which point they would live together as husband and wife, on their own land. They would be the wealthiest family in town, he assured her.

Pista read the letter twice and set it down. Pini was so different from the Ruganis. Beppe and Cecco had their edges, but at heart they were kind. She was not so sure the same could be said for Faustino Pini. She was glad to have some time before confronting the reality of his return.

Tensions had been simmering in the Rugani household since the disclosure of Pista's and Cecco's liaison. The family carried on with the work of the farm, but the previous light and loving spirit was gone. Visiting Loppeglia one day, Teopista told the whole sad story to her mother, and it was the practical Felice who came up with an idea.

"Pista," she said, "you need to get away from all this. Here is an advertisement in the newspaper for a family in Pisa in need of a wet nurse. The timing is perfect. Take your children and go to Pisa. You will feel better with some time in a different situation."

Teopista felt a glimmer of interest for the first time in months. She could finally get out of town as the men did so easily, and see something new. She kissed her mother and immediately wrote to the family in Pisa. Within days, she, Iolanda, and baby Beppino were packed and on their way to Pisa by horse and wagon. It was not more than twenty miles, but farther than Teopista had ever traveled in her life. She was exhilarated.

Wealthy families in Tuscany treated their wet nurses very

well, to ensure nutritious milk for the baby. Teopista and her children lived in the elegant home of her employer and received ample quantities of good food. She missed her family and Cecco back at home, and she could not banish her worries about the impending return of Faustino Pini, but for a few months Pista's life was easier than it had ever been. Her sole responsibilities were to nurse the babies and care for Iolanda. She sat in the family's outdoor courtyard, with one child on each breast and Iolanda playing nearby, and soaked in the view of the red-tiled rooftops of Pisa, punctuated by domed steeples and the famous leaning tower. Every hour churchbells rang out in a clanging cacophony. Pista closed her eyes and let the complications of her life recede into the distant hills like the trailing off of the bells.

The reprieve was short-lived. By midsummer 1909, the babies were weaned and Teopista was released from service in Pisa. She brought her children back to the Marchi home, feeling refreshed but now anxious all over again. Faustino's return was imminent.

As the town of Torcigliano Alto had done when the Rugani brothers came home, so the people of Loppeglia rushed out to greet Faustino Pini, overwhelming him with hugs, cheers, and tears. Villagers hosted a feast out in the piazza, and begged Faustino for stories of America, which he was only too glad to provide. As he regaled them with one tale after another, most of which were at least half true, his audience hung on every word.

Teopista and Felice watched Faustino become puffed up with all the attention, and knew this was the best possible way to soften him up for the news he had not yet heard. As the two had planned, Teopista brought only three-year-old Iolanda to the celebrations, while her sister Corradina stayed in the Marchi home with baby Beppino. Faustino swept his daughter off her feet and lifted her over his head. "My beautiful girl! You have no idea how much I missed you!" He kissed her forehead and whirled the confused little girl around. Her mother had told her that her father was coming home, but this strange man frightened her. She started to cry, which made Faustino laugh.

"Yes, I am a stranger to you now, but not for long. Soon we will be the best of friends, my magnificent daughter." He set Iolanda back down on the ground and she ran full-speed back to her mother's arms.

"It's okay, *cara*. This is your father," said Teopista, adding generously, "He loves you very much."

That night Pista couldn't bear to ruin the celebratory mood, so she left Beppino with Corradina and maintained her deception. Faustino seemed almost like a stranger, it had been so long, but he was full of adrenaline and pride from all the attention he'd received, and she could not refuse him when he finally came to bed in the early hours of the morning. Her body was present, but her mind was racing: *What is he going to do when he finds out about the baby? How will I tell him?* Usually an expert at handling such moments, Pista could think of no good outcome in this case, and she spent most of the night worrying.

As she had done before with her mercurial husband, Pista chose a moment when Faustino was relaxed and happy, and when his family was present to moderate his reaction. After dinner at the Pinis' home, she arranged for Corradina to bring the baby over. Pista took a deep breath. "*Faustino, mio marito,* I want you to meet the baby Giuseppe."

Faustino smiled with delight. "A baby! Congratulations, Corradina! Your son is beautiful."

Corradina and the whole family looked over at Pista. "Actually," she said slowly, "this is not Corradina's baby. He is mine. Ours. This is Giuseppe Vincenzo Pini, your son."

"What?" Faustino stared at his wife. "What?!" He slammed his hand down on the table. "This is not possible!" He jumped out of his seat. "What the hell have you done? *Putana!*" He fell silent for a moment. "You whore." The door slammed behind him as he left the house.

No one said anything for a long moment. Pista cradled her baby in her arms and closed her eyes. "Corradina," she said finally, "let's go home."

She did not see her husband for the next three days. When he finally returned to Loppeglia, he looked terrible. He had been drinking in Monsagrati, drowning his sorrows and fuming.

"Pista," he said to her, "what you have done is unforgiveable. I renounce you as my wife. I am going back to America to get rich, and you will be sorry for your betrayal. You will never enjoy the life of a rich woman, ever, in your life." With that, Faustino Pini headed directly back to the coast to purchase a ticket to America, identifying himself to the ticketing agent as an unmarried man.

"So that's how it's going to be, Mama." Teopista said to Felice. "Your daughter is a disgraced woman, with two children named Pini."

Felice nodded, calm as always in the face of family drama.

"The thing is," Pista said, "I'm trying to feel bad about all this, but I don't. I feel better than I have in months. Is that wrong?"

"Oh, Pista. You are my irrepressible girl. Should you feel remorseful? Maybe. But if you don't, you don't. The only thing that really matters is that you raise those children with the love and security they deserve. They need their mother's full attention. Do you understand?"

"Of course I do, Mama. I would sacrifice everything to do what's best for Iolanda and Beppino." And so, with an absolution of sorts from her mother, Teopista kneaded dough for the day's bread for her family. A bubble of joy arose unbidden in her heart.

Upon Teopista's return from her stint as a wet nurse in Pisa, the Marchis had made room in their crowded house for her and the children. Everyone adored the baby Beppino, but he kept the household awake at night with his crying, and the large family was packed in like *sardine*. It was also awkward, for the first time ever, for Teopista to be in such close proximity to Faustino's family. In a small village, there's no escape when neighbors have a falling out. The Pinis did still love Teopista—it was impossible not to love her—but they blamed her for the rapid departure of their Faustino, before they had even really seen him. And the presence of baby Beppino, just two doors down, was a constant reminder of their daughter-in-law's infidelity. The tension between Pinis and Marchis was palpable.

While Iolanda played with the younger Marchi children, Teopista began to take long walks with Beppino strapped to her chest. It was a relief to get out of the village, and the exercise felt good. One afternoon she headed down to Monsagrati, and, on an impulse, turned toward the road to Torcigliano Alto. Breathing the sweet air, her steps grew more decisive. She would go see the Ruganis. Francesco would be happy to see his son, and she missed the family she had come to love nearly as much as her own. The baby grew heavy on her chest as she climbed the long hill, but Teopista was too exhilarated to care.

"Pista!" The Rugani women rushed out of the house, embracing her and pulling baby Beppino out of his cloth wrap. Rosa brewed coffee and produced a plate of her famous biscotti, while the Rugani girls tickled the baby and laughed every time he did.

"We miss you, Pista," said Rosa. "It was not right, what you and Cecco did, but we miss you. And Iolanda. Where is our girl? You did not bring her?"

"Not today, Rosa. Actually, I didn't know myself that I would come up here until I was on the road. I suddenly just needed to see you." Teopista tilted her head back and smiled. It felt so good to be back in Torcigliano and away from the Pinis. A moment later she heard a familiar voice outside the house. Cecco.

Cecco's sister had found him out on a terrace and called him to come home. He had run all the way and was out of breath. "Pista, you are here! And where is my boy? Where is Giuseppe Vincenzo?" He lifted the baby and kissed him all over. "Beppino, you are the most beautiful boy who ever lived." Francesco looked so delighted with his son in his arms that even Rosa had to smile.

"Stay with us tonight, Pista. Dionisio and Beppe will want to see you, too." There was no way to send a message home to her mother, but Teopista had no intention of saying no. She would go home in the morning and tell Felice where she'd been.

At supper, everyone talked at once. Time had softened the jealousy and anger of the previous year, and the family was ready to laugh. After a couple of glasses of wine, Pista got up and sang and danced, making eye contact with every person around the table. She had not felt so good in a long time.

She still felt a glow the next morning as she kissed the family goodbye and set out for home with Beppino on her chest. Nearly-ripe olives hung on the trees. Soon it would be harvest time. Warm sunshine permeated her soul, and Pista hummed in her son's ear all the way down the hill to Monsagrati and back up to Loppeglia.

Not even two days later came a knock on the Marchis' door. It was a replay of the scene from a year and a half earlier, but this time both Rugani brothers stood politely outside, perspiring from the exertion of their walk. "Beppe and Cecco, come in," Felice welcomed them. "Corradina, go get your father. Tell him we have company."

The Ruganis had come with a proposal. They wanted Teopista and both her children to come back to live with them in Torcigliano Alto. Rosa needed the help, everyone loved the children, and the bad feelings of the year before had faded. "May we have your permission?" Giuseppe asked Felice and Adolfo.

"My daughter," said Adolfo to Pista, "this is no longer our decision to make. You are an adult and the mother of two children. You know the situation here, and it is up to you to do as you wish."

Teopista could not disguise her joy. She looked back and forth at Giuseppe and Francesco and couldn't decide which one she loved more. The prospect of living with them both was intoxicating. "Mama and Papa, I will love you forever and will come see you every week, but yes I will move back to Torcigliano Alto. The Ruganis need my help, and they are devoted to little Iolanda and Beppino. This will be good for us."

She hugged her parents and turned to Beppe and Cecco. "Tell Rosa and Dionisio that my answer is *sì!* I will come, with pleasure. *Grazie mille.*"

This time, Teopista promised herself to resist the temptation to sneak off to the upper terrace. It really was true that she loved both brothers, and she did not want to hurt Giuseppe as she had before. She found that it was almost as much fun to flirt equally with both of them as it had been to satisfy her physical desire with Cecco. She privately enjoyed driving them both a little crazy, in a miniature replay of her days dancing in Monsagrati for a plaza full of admiring men. And although it was less thrilling, the choice to be honest was satisfying in a deeper way. Pista was having fun yet doing right by both brothers, and the entire household could tell.

They had their moments. Cecco could not always control his jealousy when he saw Teopista paying flirty attention to Beppe. He would withdraw and sulk until she teased him back to life. Giuseppe never fully got over the betrayal he felt over his brother's liaison with Pista, either, and there was a baby in his face every day to remind him. He was honored to have a namesake, but never could love baby Beppino with his whole heart.

For her part, Teopista occasionally indulged in some melancholy. Where was her life going? She was married to an absent man she didn't love, and she loved two other men but couldn't choose either one without upsetting the whole close-knit family. The situation was a trap, albeit a happy one. Most days she suppressed these thoughts and joked with Rosa as they cooked and cleaned.

Late autumn of 1911 yielded a bumper crop of olives. All family members worked to exhaustion picking fruit and pressing oil, and as always watched the liquid gold be carted away by their landowner. Their tenant status rankled, and Beppe and

Cecco began to revive their dream of one day owning their own orchards. As their conversations took on increasing urgency, Teopista understood that life was again about to change. She wondered what it would mean this time.

For the brothers, the question of whether or not to go to America was very different this second time around. Instead of a great adventure, the journey was a known quantity. The back-breaking work of a trammer underground was dangerous and didn't pay well. Who wouldn't rather be out in the Tuscan sunshine tending vineyards and olive orchards? And yet, there was no way out from under the landowner's thumb without earning money, and no way to earn money without leaving home.

By Italian custom, the oldest son is responsible for taking care of the parents and tending the *casa paterna,* the family home. In exchange, he will inherit this home one day. Dionisio and Rosa were getting older, and Giuseppe did not feel right leaving them on their own. Brother number three had married and moved away, so Dionisio didn't have as much help as he had had when Beppe went to America the first time. After hours of discussion, the brothers reached an agreement: Francesco would return to Baltic, Michigan, to earn more money, while Giuseppe stayed home and cared for his parents and the *casa paterna.* This time they knew how much money they needed to buy land, and as soon as Cecco had that amount, he would return home.

To channel their sadness, Rosa and Teopista packed Cecco a bag of food so large he could barely lift it. Giuseppe insisted his brother take enough money to buy a second-class ticket, to avoid the miserable, stinking steerage compartment. And Dionisio put his big hands on Francesco's shoulders. "I could not ask for a better son. You are doing a wonderful thing for your family, and I am proud of you. We will pray for you every day and have a great celebration when you return. Thank you, my son."

Buoyed by all this love, Francesco tearfully hugged each member of the family. He gave Beppino, about to be three years old, an embrace so tight that the boy gasped. When it was Teopista's turn, Cecco memorized every detail of her face. "I will think of you every day and dream of you every night," he whispered." She put her hand over the locket containing the photographs they took in Lucca, and smiled through her tears. "God be with you, Cecco. We will be here, waiting for you."

God apparently was with Francesco, because he missed his boat. He was booked to board in Cherbourg, France, on April 10, 1912, but his train to Cherbourg arrived too late. The ship he missed was the RMS *Titanic*. He arrived safely in America on a subsequent steamship, and for the rest of his life he kept a newspaper clipping about the sinking of the *Titanic* in his prayer book.

With Francesco gone, the household dynamics in Torcigliano Alto shifted yet again. Giuseppe worked side by side with his father, taking increasing responsibility for the workings of the farm. Teopista spent her days cleaning and cooking with Rosa and caring for her children. Each mid-day, as the family gathered for their big meal, the younger Ruganis chattered about school, the men discussed the condition of the orchards, and everyone hoped for a bit of good gossip to filter back from Monsagrati. It was not until evening that the adults had some time to themselves, and Teopista and Giuseppe resumed their old habit of talking, joking, and enjoying one another's company.

Teopista had grown accustomed to sublimating her feelings for the Rugani brothers, and she drew on this discipline now. Evenings with Beppe were an enjoyable way to end the day, and nothing more. Pista could make any member of the Rugani family laugh, and she relished the challenge of coming up with just the right joke for each person. On Saturdays they set off down the hill to Monsagrati, for errands and socializing. Pista still loved to dance, the bigger the audience the better. She also loved her regular visits with her family, watching Iolanda and her nursing-sister, Ersilia, play together, and telling her mother about the details of life in Torcigliano Alto.

Unlike Faustino Pini, Cecco wrote regular letters home. He was being paid a bit more than last time, due to his greater experience, but a trammer's pay was still terrible. The mine-workers, he told the family, were dissatisfied. The owners were rich and the managers did well, but the men underground barely made a living. "I found out," Cecco wrote, "that the managers try to keep us from talking too much to each other by mixing up Italians with Croatians, Russians, and others who don't speak our language. They think we won't figure out what's happening. But some of the Italians who've been here the longest have learned English and made connections. There is talk of forming a union."

Men underground were severely injured, or even killed, on a regular basis. "There are drills operated by just one man now," Cecco told his family. "No one is there to help if there's an accident. The drillers are really angry about this. My trammer's job is not as dangerous, but it's backbreaking and the pay is horrible. But, *mia famiglia,* do not worry. I am saving every penny so I can come home to you. Beppe, we will buy our orchard and life will be good! This is a temporary situation."

In August 2013 came a serious letter. "Dear Papa, Mama, and Giuseppe, On July 23, we voted to strike for higher wages and better working conditions. Mines all over the area are shut down. I hope this will not last long."

Cecco's hopes were not realized, as the Copper Country miners' strike dragged on for months, testing the willpower of both sides. The workers held remarkably firm, given their ethnic diversity and their desperate need for income. Union leaders urged them to stay the course, promising that safer conditions and more money would result. This strategy had worked for miners in the western United States and it would work here in Michigan, too, the organizers promised, so the workers gritted their teeth, walked the picket line, and waited.

Francesco was torn. He understood the complaints of his fellow workers, but by nature he was not a protester. Miners willing to tear up their union cards were given their jobs back, and enough men had done this that some of the mines were operating on a limited basis. Cecco hated the idea of betraying his fellow workers on strike, yet going back to work was the only way to save money for the orchard. After some sleepless nights of indecision, he tore up his union card and sheepishly crossed the picket line.

In early January 1914, the Ruganis gathered to read Cecco's latest letter. The news was horrifying. On Christmas Eve 1913, there had been a huge party in the Italian Hall in nearby Calumet, Michigan. Families gathered for some badly needed festivities, a respite from the pressures of the strike. Suddenly someone yelled, "Fire!" into the crowded room, and a stampede ensued. Seventy-three men, women, and children were crushed to death in a stairway. There was no fire.

Italians on both sides of the Atlantic were shocked. Cecco was not at the party and he didn't know any of the victims personally, but he was deeply shaken by the tragedy. "Can you imagine how awful this is for those poor families?" he wrote. "Some people are saying it was done on purpose, to intimidate the strikers. It is not usual for me to think this way, but I have to admit it could be true."

Giuseppe wrote back to his brother. "Cecco, everyone here is talking about the Italian Hall tragedy. We are so worried. Please be careful, and consider coming home."

Thousands of miners left the Copper Country during the long winter of 1914. They needed work to survive, tensions were at a peak, and the strike showed no signs of ending. Cecco read Beppe's letter and did think about whether to go home. Every morning, when he scuttled across the picket line, he felt embarrassed and afraid. There were frequent fistfights between angry union men and strikebreakers like him. At the same time, he worried about the union busters rumored to have been behind the Italian Hall massacre. What else might they do? Should he leave the Upper Peninsula and look for work elsewhere? Cecco didn't know where he would go, and as unhappy as he was, he hated even more the thought of going home without the money he'd promised his family he would earn. He decided to stay.

In Torcigliano Alto, the Ruganis worried about Cecco every day. When he wrote in February that he had decided to remain in Baltic, Rosa became so anxious she made herself sick. She took to her bed and stopped eating. Not even Teopista could cajole her back to health.

"We must do something, both for Cecco and for Rosa!" Pista addressed the family after supper one evening. "I have an idea. I will go to America and bring Cecco back."

"You will do no such thing," responded Dionisio. "You have two small children and you are needed here more than ever, with Rosa the way she is. That is not the answer." The family fell silent.

"I could go," said Carlo, the youngest Rugani brother at fifteen. Everyone laughed, but quieted down when they saw the hopeful look on his face.

"My son," said Dionisio, "thank you for this offer, but we need you here, too. Here is what we will do: Each of us will take turns going to Rosa's bed. Tell her we need her back, tell her a story to make her laugh, say a prayer with her, and do whatever you can think of to convince her to come back to us. Meanwhile we will carry on with our work. No one else will go to America. Do you understand?"

Everyone nodded and the family carried on. The work of the farm continued, but emotions remained heightened and still Rosa did not rise from her bed. Giuseppe and Teopista's nighttime conversations were a refuge for them both, and as time passed, Pista found herself relying on Beppe more and more. He was her confidante and her closest companion, and they began staying up later and later, not wanting to say goodnight.

On one of those very late nights, they stood up reluctantly to head off to bed. Their eyes met, and suddenly Beppe stepped forward instead of back. He pulled Pista in and kissed her. She responded with urgency, but quickly disengaged. "Beppe, no. We must not."

"I know," he said, "it was a mistake. We will not speak of this again."

Not long after the arrival of Cecco's letter, another envelope arrived, addressed to Teopista Marchi. To her utter surprise, it was from Faustino Pini. Pini was also a miner in Baltic, Michigan, and the Italian Hall disaster had hit him very close to home. As an active union member, he told Pista, he had almost attended that party in Calumet on Christmas Eve, but stayed home at the last minute. "I could have been killed!" he wrote. "I have been able to think of only two things since then—the terrible wrong that was done to Italians by those anti-union scum, and the need to have my family—my wife and daughter—here with me. Pista, I was very angry with you for what you did, but I want to give you another chance. Come here with Iolanda and we will live together as a family in Michigan. Leave that bastard son where he belongs, and come be with your rightful husband. I will forgive you and love you as if the betrayal never happened. Pista, *mia moglie,* my wife, I miss you. Please come. Your husband, Faustino Pini."

Pista set the letter down on the table, her mind churning. *How dare he call my Beppino a bastard? He's the one who's a bastard! Does he think in a million years I would leave my sweet son?* Pista closed her eyes. What she wanted most was to talk this over with Beppe, but she could not. She had to think it through for herself. *It would be an adventure to move to America. What about that? Maybe this is my chance to see the world and do something besides bake bread and clean the house. But—the only way I would even consider going would be with both my children. Faustino would just have to accept it. But would I do it? I do not love Faustino any more, and I am needed here. Yet he is my husband—do I owe it to him to try again?*

To calm herself down, Teopista poured a big glass of wine. She could not deny, privately, that there would be another advantage to moving to Baltic, Michigan. She would see Cecco. Faustino would try to keep them apart, but she would find ways to see Cecco, and she could write home to Rosa and the family to tell them how he was faring. It was so hard to tell, just from letters. Teopista's heart and mind, both, were divided. She decided to take her time and think, without replying right away to Faustino.

Meanwhile, she faced the intensity of what had happened with Beppe. They tried to disguise the awkwardness between them, but Pista could not stop thinking about that kiss. It was obvious that they desired each other, but the liaison was unwise. Pista had to get her irrepressible emotions under control. She was exuberant by nature, but with men, she simply could not act with abandon, especially in the wake of her husband's letter. She promised herself to pull back.

Her resolve didn't last. Night after night she headed off to bed early, only to toss and turn on her cornhusk mattress. Then came a warm spring afternoon. Pista was outside with Iolanda and Beppino when Giuseppe appeared, asking if he could speak with her. Pista put the babies under twelve-year-old Alaide Rugani's care, and headed off to walk with Beppe. As soon as they were out of sight and sound of the farm, Beppe said, "Pista, I can't stand it. Please say that I may kiss you again, or I will go crazy."

Pista melted. She sank into Giuseppe's arms and simply gave way. It was her nature. She was too happy and desirous to care about the complications. That night she placed her locket lovingly in Francesco's trunk of belongings, and she wrote to Faustino that she had decided not to go to America.

In Michigan's Copper Country, the strike finally came to an end in April 1914, nine months after it began. Union ranks were decimated by all the workers who had left the area, and most of their demands were rejected. The workday was shortened to eight hours and wages for trammers and miners went up a bit, due to new labor laws, but there would be no collective bargaining and no banning of the one-man drill. It was not a happy outcome, but Francesco was relieved not to have to cross the picket line any more. His pay was better, though still low, and his body had more time to recover with an eight-hour day. He wrote home to tell the family the strike was over and he was fine.

Everyone breathed easier in the Rugani household. Rosa got out of bed and the whole family went down to Monsagrati on Saturday night to celebrate the end of the strike. When the music started, Teopista pulled eight-year-old Iolanda out on the dance floor and spun her around. "Watch this!" she said to her laughing daughter, and she settled a wine bottle on her pinned-up hair.

"Woo hoo!" Men in the piazza whistled and cheered as Pista played the crowd, swaying and winking just like the old days. Giuseppe watched from the sidelines, quietly certain that he would be the beneficiary of all this exuberance when they returned home that night.

A new normal settled in at the Rugani home after that. Pista and Beppe carried on their semi-clandestine affair, which everyone knew about but no one discussed. Pista became pregnant once, but miscarried. Letters came from Francesco, telling stories of boarding house life and his slowly growing savings. The family read each one out loud in the evening, savoring every word.

A steady stream of letters also came from Faustino Pini, which Pista did not read out loud. Her refusal of his first request had spurred Faustino on to more passionate and flattering approaches.

Although she did not reply to the letters, Pista had to admit his pleas had an effect. Her affair with Giuseppe was a welcome diversion, but as one year turned into a second, Teopista felt herself growing restless. Daily life in the Rugani household was pleasant but repetitive. She was twenty-eight years old, full of life and energy, and what were her prospects in Torcigliano Alto? Would she grow old as an unmarried mother and domestic servant? Would she never see anything more of the world?

Once an idea took hold with Teopista, it didn't take long to harden into resolve. She had not discussed the option of moving to America with anyone, including her mother, but one day in the autumn of 1915, she knew she had decided to go. Her announcement came as an absolute shock to three families: the Ruganis, the Marchis, and the Pinis.

"Pista," said Felice, "are you very sure?"

"Yes, Mama, I am sure. I want to see the world. Why is it only the men who travel to America? I am still married, despite everything, and Faustino swears he will treat me like a queen when I arrive."

Felice regarded her daughter much as she had ten years

before when Teopista decided to marry. "You have always followed your own mind and heart, *cara*. I am concerned you will not be happy, and I will miss you more than I can say, but I know better than to try to change your mind. Go to America, may God be with you."

Pista suddenly realized how much she would miss her mother's unconditional embrace, and her eyes filled. "Thank you, Mama. I love you so much."

The other painful conversation took place with Giuseppe Rugani. He was desolate at the prospect of Teopista's departure. "Oh, Pista," he said to her, as they lay together in November for the last time. "What will I do without you?"

"Beppe," she said, "you are many things to me—my friend, my lover, and almost like a brother. I will miss you terribly. But we both know we have no real future together. I am married to Pini, for better or worse, and I have borne a child with Cecco. You need to find a woman you can marry, and start your own proper family. This is what you must do, and I will no longer hold you back from the future you deserve." She had not planned to say all this, but as the words came out of her mouth, Teopista knew she was right. She needed to go, not just for her own sake, but for Giuseppe's. They both began to cry.

"Pista, I am afraid I'll never see you again," said Beppe, through his tears.

"Don't be silly, *caro*. Nothing could keep me from my beloved home forever. But, you know, it will be different for us. I will be the wife of Faustino Pini when I return." Teopista swallowed. She prayed she was doing the right thing; the only way to find out was to go.

Across the ocean and half a continent away, Faustino was overjoyed. He had won his wife back. He could give up the desperate whorehouses visited by unmarried men in South Range, and come home each night to his beautiful, sexy Teopista. He was a very long way from rich, but he moved out of the boarding house and rented a company duplex home on 13th Avenue, in the Italian section of town, for himself, Teopista, and Iolanda. Then he had a big idea, a way to show his wife what a successful man he was. He would meet her at the station in a horse and buggy! The Lucchesi Livery Stable was run by a family from the same region of Tuscany, and Pini knew they would rent him an impressive rig. Yes, this was just right. They would ride home in style.

In Torcigliano Alto, Teopista was full of energy. She secured the necessary paperwork to travel to America with her two children, and she packed their belongings into two stuffed suitcases. Then she made the rounds of friends and family to say goodbye. At each home, Pista was plied with coffee, sandwiches, and biscotti, and sent off with tearful hugs and kisses. She was known and loved in at least three separate towns, so these visits were numerous and fattening. Again, Pista prayed she was doing the right thing. How could she leave behind all these dear people? Or, for that matter, the beauty and fragrance of home? It wasn't too late to change her mind, but despite her waves of doubt, she resolved to go. Whatever lay in store for her and the children, it would be an adventure.

The most painful farewell came on the last day, when she had to part with her mother. Pista sobbed so hard in Felice's arms that Iolanda and Beppino, ages nine and six, became upset. When her children started to wail, Teopista realized she had to pull herself together. She had successfully gotten them excited about the grand adventure they were about to undertake, and now she was upsetting them with her tears. She wiped her face on her sleeve, put a smile on her face, and enveloped her children in a hug. "My darlings, everything is fine. Sometimes people are happy and sad at the same time. It's sad to say goodbye, but it's time to board our ship and sail to America, and this is very exciting. *Andiamo!* Let's go!"

Baltic and South Range, Michigan

Teopista, Iolanda, and Beppino Pini traveled second-class to New York in November 1915. Iolanda and Beppino spent every possible moment out on the deck of the ship, watching for fish and chattering with children of other families who were equally thrilled by the experience. Teopista enjoyed their pleasure, but the rolling waves didn't agree with her. She took deep breaths and tried to calm her stomach, with only moderate success. It was a relief to at last reach Ellis Island.

After hearing the stories of Cecco and Beppe Rugani, Pista knew what to expect in New York. She told her children they would wait in long lines and be examined for health before they could board the train to Chicago. Beppino was a delicate child, but he passed the exams along with his robust sister and mother, and they were granted admission to America.

The children openly gaped at the strange sights and sounds. *"Mama! Guarda! Guarda le enormi edifice!* Look at the huge buildings!" Pista's eyes were nearly as wide as her children's. *"Sì, bambini.* We are on an adventure." As the train chugged its way out of New York and headed west, the overstimulated children finally grew quiet. Their heads tilted back and mouths dropped open as they sank into deep sleep.

Teopista badly needed rest as well, but she barely dozed. In part, she was keeping a mother's vigilant eye on her children, but there was something else. The queasiness she had attributed to seasickness on the ship had not fully receded. She hoped it was the motion of the train that kept her stomach on edge, but in her heart she knew better. She spent the long trip to Chicago coming to terms with the truth that not only was she about to reveal to Faustino Pini that she had brought both children with her, but also that she was pregnant. *Dio mi aiuti!* God help me, she thought. Pista calculated that she wouldn't have to tell Faustino about the pregnancy right away. She was less than two months along—maybe she'd have a miscarriage and Pini would never know. Otherwise, she would take as much time as she could get away with, letting the dust settle from the arrival of Beppino along with Iolanda. None of this would be easy, but Teopista would get through it one way or another. What choice did she have? *Si fa come si puole, non come si vuole,* she told herself. We do what we must do and not what we want to do.

From Chicago they were booked on trains that led to South Range, Michigan, the neighboring town to Baltic in the Upper Peninsula's Copper Country. Iolanda and Beppino's noses were pressed flat against the window as they watched the landscape change. Chicago felt a bit like New York, but as soon as they left the city they were rolling through fallow November fields, flatter than anything they'd seen at home. Milwaukee was a cacophony of steam engines and belching factories, and then it was back to cows and brown fields. America was so big!

Teopista had practiced the sound of the English words "South Range," to be sure she knew when to get off the train. She had the children and their bags ready long in advance, as she sounded out the strange sounds over and over to herself. *"Souta Reincia."* Suddenly there it was: "South Range!" called the engineer. "South Range next!"

Pista and her children joined the line of people and bags in the aisle. The train was packed with men headed for work in the mines. Only a handful of women and children accompanied them. Teopista took a deep breath. What was this strange place she had agreed to live in? How would she and her children fit into a world of mining men?

On the platform it took a moment for Faustino Pini to find his wife and daughter. When he saw them he pressed through the crowd, yelling so loudly that heads turned: "Pista! Pista!"

"My wife is here!" he told several strangers. Faustino was making the most of his proud moment. He would now join the echelon of mining men with families, no longer stuck in the bachelor-sad boarding house. Pini swept his wife and daughter to him in an exuberant embrace, kissing them on both cheeks and gripping their hands with pleasure. "Let me take your bags.

I have a surprise for you!" he said. "Follow me!"

"Faustino," said Teopista, "Wait. First you must say hello to your son, Giuseppe. You have not seen him in six years, during which time he has grown into a magnificent boy."

Pini had not noticed—or had pretended not to notice—the pale boy standing on the platform next to Iolanda. He turned to Teopista with fire in his eyes. "Pista," he hissed. "How could you?"

"How could I not, Faustino? You think I would abandon my son? Never!" Teopista was ready for this moment. "My husband, please trust that this is the right thing. Tell the world that this is your beautiful son, and welcome him just as you welcome Iolanda and me. You will see that he is a good boy. And more, I have a feeling about him. I think he has a special gift, something that will make us proud. I don't know what it is yet, but my heart tells me so."

Pini closed his eyes. He had just enough decency not to explode in the presence of the children, and too much pride to make a scene on the crowded platform. He flashed a look at Beppino and said, "Come along, then. Let's go home."

Not one to waste an opportunity to be in the limelight, Faustino supressed his anger and grandly showed his family to their carriage. Pista laughed. "This is for us? How wonderful, Faustino!" She had not forgotten how to flatter her husband. The four of them rode in style from the train station to their new home on 13th Avenue in Baltic. Pista and her children pulled up a lap blanket to shield themselves from the November cold, and stared at every detail.

"Mama," said Beppino, "why is the ground white? What is wrong with it?"

Faustino laughed. "Nothing is wrong," he said over his shoulder from the driver's seat. "This is snow. And I hope you like it, because you will see a whole lot more before this winter is over. I will show you what you can do with it."

"Mama, it's so cold here," said Iolanda.

"I know, *cara*. We will make warm coats and hats and mittens. And we will all need boots for our feet." Teopista drew her daughter closer under the blanket. What she was noticing, in addition to the strange snow, was how busy the town of South Range was. More than 1,200 people lived there, supported by food stores, blacksmiths, laundry, and seamstresses. Horses and pedestrians shared the road with a few carriages like the one they rode in. The town felt more like Lucca than tiny Loppeglia, though much colder and not at all as charming. To her relief, Pista heard Italian spoken on the street. One of her greatest fears had been the inability to communicate, but South Range was home to many Italian miners and families. *Take it one step at a time,* she told herself. *You are contadina. You can do this.*

Baltic, the community just to the southeast, was a little smaller but also included an Italian neighborhood. Pini pulled the carriage up in front of a small wooden duplex and the family stepped down. "Welcome to your new home," said Faustino. "There is no bed for the boy, so he will sleep on the floor."

"His name is Beppino and no, he will not sleep on the floor," said Teopista calmly. "Beppino and Iolanda will share a bed. Okay, children?" They looked down at the floor and nodded.

In the ensuing weeks, Teopista got her children enrolled in the Baltic Elementary School. Kind Italian neighbor women showed her where to shop and invited her for coffee. They loaned her warm clothing until she was able to sew winter garments for the children and herself. She would have been lost without their help, but many Italians she met had come from the same region of Lucca, and they all remembered the shock of arriving in this strange place. They especially remembered the challenges of their first winter. The cold and snow never stopped. *Orribile!* Horrible! "You get used to it," they told Pista, "but you never like it. The men get to go underground where it's warmer, but that's not so great either. There are accidents, and you never know whether your man will come back at night or not."

Grateful for her new friends, Teopista quickly endeared herself to them by letting her ebullient personality show. She invited new friends into her home. "Let's have a party on

Saturday night!" she said. Neighbors came over to sing and dance, and Faustino Pini glowed with pride.

Teopista and her children were getting used to their peculiar new home, and Pini seemed resigned to the presence of young Beppino, but as the winter dragged on, Pista began to gain weight. She hid her condition under layers of cold-weather clothing, but she worried that Pini would notice when he came to her at night. She could not put off the inevitable conversation forever, and one February morning she woke up determined to tell him that evening.

"Faustino," she said softly, after plying her husband with wine, "I have news."

"*Sì*, Pista, what is it?"

"We are going to have a baby."

"How wonderful! I hope it will be a boy, so I can have a *real* son." Faustino kissed his wife. "When will this little miracle be born?"

Teopista swallowed. "In June, *caro.*"

Faustino pulled back. "June?" He stared at Pista. "June!" He said nothing for a long, simmering moment, and then he got up and paced around the room.

"*Puttana!* I can't believe it. Who is the father? Francesco was over here last fall, so it's not that piece of scum. Who is it?"

Teopista said nothing. "Let's talk when you calm down, Faustino."

Faustino did not calm down. He paced and ran his hands through his hair all night long, and left for work in the morning in silence. Teopista did not sleep, either. She longed for her mother, who would know what to say, or at least would comfort her, but Felice was thousands of miles away. Pista felt more alone than she ever had in her life, lying pregnant in her empty bed, deep into a Michigan winter.

Faustino did not come home until very late the next night. Teopista feigned sleep and listened as her husband opened and closed drawers. It sounded like he was stuffing clothing into a bag, and then he stomped back down the stairs and slammed the door.

Each day Teopista expected Pini to return, but he did not. She was relieved not to have to face his anger, but surely he would come back soon. She waited and worried.

A week after Faustino's departure, there was a knock on her door. It was a mining company representative.

"Mrs. Pini?"

"*Sì*, yes. What is it?"

"Your husband has not been to work in a week. Is he here?"

Teopista understood just enough of the question to shake her head. "Pini no here," she said.

"Where is he?" asked the man.

"*Non lo so.* I don't know."

"Well, ma'am, if he has left, you cannot live here any more. This is a company house."

Teopista needed to be sure she understood. She put up a finger and asked the man to wait. She ran next door and knocked on her neighbor's door. "Rosina, can you help me? A man is here and I do not understand him."

Rosina listened to the company man's message and translated. "He says if Pini is not coming back, you have to leave the house."

Teopista's eyes widened. She had no idea their home was supplied by the mining company. She had only been in America three months. It was freezing cold outside and the snow was three feet high.

"Sir," Rosina said, "you cannot evict this woman. She has two children and another on the way. Where would she go?"

"Not my problem, lady. The company needs this house. Tell her she has three days to get out." The company man looked Pista's neighbor in the eye. "Do you understand?"

"Yes, sir."

He turned to Teopista. "Mrs. Pini, do you understand?"

"*Sì, signore. Capisco.* I understand."

"Three days." And with that he left.

"Oh my God, Pista, I am sorry!" Rosina gave her a big hug. "I have to get back to my baby now, but let's talk later."

Pista collapsed into uncharacteristic sobs. What on earth

would she do in this strange place, in the winter, with no place to live and no income? After a cathartic cry, she pulled herself together and considered her options. It was not possible to stay with any of her new friends for more than a day or two. No one in Baltic or South Range would have room for a family of three, soon to be four, in their very small mining company accommodations. She could go back to Italy, back to the warm embrace of her mother and the Ruganis, back to the sun-drenched Tuscan terraces. But she had no money for tickets, and she loathed the idea of asking for a loan. Besides, even if she did humble herself enough to ask, who would be willing to give her such a large amount? The only person she knew well enough was Francesco Rugani, whom she had not yet seen because Pini would not allow it. *But I can't ask Cecco,* Pista thought. *He is here to earn money for his orchard.*

Pista got up and walked around the small living room. She had to provide for her children, but how? It was a million miles from the scenario she had imagined for herself in America, but Pista realized she had to find a job. As a woman who spoke almost no English, had nowhere to live, and was pregnant, such a thing seemed impossible, even for a *contadina*. Teopista went back over to Rosina's house and knocked on the door.

"Rosina, I'm sorry to bother you again."

"Teopista, don't even think it. Sit, have a glass of wine, and we will talk. Italians look out for one another here."

By the time her wine glass was empty, Pista had agreed to go with Rosina to see Dominick Zana in South Range. Zana knew everyone. "He will help if he likes you," Rosina told Teopista, "so turn on the charm and wait until he's in a good mood before you ask him for anything."

Charm was Teopista's specialty. She had Dominick Zana laughing within ten minutes of meeting him and, as Rosina had predicted, she left with an offer of help. "Go see the Bassos," he said. "They run a boarding house here in South Range, and Donata is overworked. Tell them I sent you."

"Oh, my God." Donata Basso listened to Teopista's story and shook her head. 'Those company men are criminal. Here's the thing: I do need help here, but every corner of the house is occupied. The only place I could offer you and your children to sleep is in the barn. It's warm at night with the animals breathing, and the hay will be comfortable under your blankets, but there's no denying it is a barn. What do you think?"

Pista didn't hesitate. "I'll take it. And I'll work hard for you, Mrs. Basso. *Grazie,* thank you." She kissed Donata's hand. "You won't regret this." Outside the door she hugged Rosina. "You have saved me, my friend. *Grazie mille.*"

When Pista told Iolanda and Beppino that they would be sleeping in a barn, they stared at her. "Mama! We are not animals!"

"Children, you are still young, but let me tell you something that will help you for the rest of your life: Sometimes we do what we must do, not what we want to do. *Si fa come si puole, non come si vuole.* Your father is gone, and we cannot stay in this house without him. By the grace of God, Mrs. Basso has offered me a job and a place for us to live. Yes, we will sleep in her barn, but it will be dry and safe. Think of it as a game. You get to sleep in a big room kept warm by cows! Nobody else at your school can do that—and yes, you will change to the school in South Range and make new friends. This is all part of our adventure. Let's make it fun."

Iolanda and Beppino were skeptical. The only thing that sounded at all good about the situation was that Faustino was gone. They had shed no tears over his departure, and hadn't even asked Teopista where he was. But to leave their school where they had just made friends, and to sleep in a barn in the middle of winter? Iolanda started to cry. "Mama, this isn't fair."

Teopista took her daughter by the shoulders. "Look me in the eye, Iolanda. I know this is hard, and I'm sorry. But please understand it could be much worse. We could be thrown out on the street in the snow, but instead we have a warm place to sleep. You will make new friends, I promise. Now get your things and get ready. It's time to go."

It snowed nearly every day in the Copper Country winter, some days just an inch or two, and other days a foot or more.

Snow on the streets was panked down by large rollers pulled by teams of horses. Men sprayed water on the packed roadway, which froze into a surface hard enough to support horse-drawn sleighs. The system worked pretty well, at least until springtime when the street devolved into a mess of ice and slush. In February, though, travel was not difficult, with pedestrians and riders and the occasional carriage passing frequently back and forth between Baltic and South Range. Teopista, Iolanda, and Beppino set out by foot in the afternoon. It was less than a mile from the Baltic apartment to Mrs. Basso's boarding house, so the walk wasn't long, but it was bitterly cold and snowing. Their teeth were chattering by the time they arrived.

Donata Basso welcomed them. "Come in, and warm yourselves by the fire. I will show you the barn and then, Teopista, if you wouldn't mind, you can help prepare supper for the returning miners and lunch pails for the departing shift." Called a "hot bed house," the Bassos' boarding house was typical of the era: Two shifts of miners took turns sleeping in the beds and eating warm meals before and after work. For the operator of the house, there were sheets to wash and change, and three meals to prepare, not just once but twice a day. Mrs. Basso was desperate for help.

Teopista put on an apron and started peeling potatoes. A dozen hungry men would soon come tromping through the door. "After you've put on the potatoes for supper," said Mrs. Basso, "dice another set of potatoes and start rolling out dough for pasties for the night shift's lunch pails." Pasties were a Cornish potato and meat pie that all ethnic groups in the Copper Country learned to prepare for their miners. They were filling, and easy to eat with no utensils. When meat was scarce, the proportion of potato, carrot, and onion went up. In the hardest times, the pasty was not much more than diced potatoes stuffed inside crust. But it filled a man's belly enough to see him through his shift.

Pista followed Mrs. Basso's instructions for the next four hours, peeling, chopping, boiling, rolling, and baking. When the day shift had eaten, the dishes had been washed, and the night shift had left the house, she sat down for the first time. Donata Basso was still at work, washing sheets from the beds of the daytime workers. She had not smiled once since Teopista and her children's arrival.

Pista saw that this job was a bit like a less loving version of her life with the Ruganis. She was needed both to work hard and to make people feel better. She could do this. "Mrs. Basso, sit. I will do the laundry. Let's talk about home." This overture drew a tired smile from Donata Basso.

A couple of days later, Teopista had an idea. "Mrs. Basso, you know what's going on now back home in Viaraggio? *Carnivale!* I used to love to put on a costume and dance and sing at this festival. Didn't you? I was thinking, why not do it here? We can dress up on Saturday night and have a party. The men will love it, and so will the children. What do you think?"

Donata shook her head, but she was smiling. "I'll give you this, Teopista. You are energetic. Okay, if you can create the costumes, make preparations, and still get your work done, I'll allow it."

Pista wasted no time. She knocked on neighbors' doors, introduced herself, and invited them to come to the boarding house on Saturday. "Wear a costume," she said, "and by the way, do you have anything I might borrow for myself and my children to wear?"

At another house she heard a violin playing. "Who is that? Please ask that musician to come play for our festival. Oh, and could you bring a little wine to share?"

By the weekend she had whipped up a party. Mrs. Basso had a piano, which more than one neighbor knew how to play. The violinist came, and so did an accordion player. The large boarding house kitchen filled up with costumed Lucchese, nostalgic for home. Throughout the evening they sang, danced, performed, ate, and drank. Even Mrs. Basso let go and enjoyed herself, exhausted and skeptical though she had been.

Teopista was in her element. Midway through the evening she picked up a straw-covered wine flask. "Iolanda, look. Do you remember what your mama used to do with one of these?

I wonder if I still can." Iolanda giggled as her mother nestled the bottle on her piled-up hair. Pista held her head level and began to sway her hips. A miner whistled. Another whooped. Pista beamed and set about working the room, her old instincts kicking in as if no time had passed. The empty bottle tilted and fell off her head, but she kept on dancing, soaking up the admiration of two dozen miners and her new neighbors.

"Iolanda, come here, *cara*. Give it a try." Pista set the bottle on her daughter's head and held it lightly. "Move your hips like so," she demonstrated. Iolanda didn't have real hips yet, but she moved left and right and tried to hold her head still, until she was laughing too hard to continue.

"Anyone else?" The neighbor women were too shy to come forward, but Teopista relaxed everyone by calling on the whole party to get up and dance. "Everybody up, now!" Pista ruled the room at that point, and the party did as she asked.

Only six-year-old Beppino did not dance. He could do nothing but stare, transfixed, at the violin player. He did not take his eyes off the musician the entire night, and before the party was over, he was imitating the movements of the violinist's hands. His intense focus did not escape his mother's attention. She had been wanting to find a way to bring her pale boy to life, and here was a clue.

"Beppino," Pista said to her son the next day, "I saw you watching the violinist last night. You liked what he was doing, no?"

"*Sì*, Mama!"

"If we can arrange it, would you like to learn to play?"

Beppino's eyes lit up. "Yes, yes, please."

"We have no money, *caro*," said Teopista, "but we will find a way. We will find an instrument and a teacher for you." Sundays were less busy at the boarding house, and that very afternoon Pista knocked on the door of the violinist's house.

"*Mi scusi, signore,* excuse me, may I ask you a question?"

"Of course, Mrs. Pini, and thank you for the best party we have had in a very long time. You brought happiness to the whole neighborhood." Mr. Rossi was beaming and Teopista knew it was the right time to ask a favor.

"*Signore*, perhaps you noticed my son last night. Beppino could not take his eyes off you and your violin. He would like to learn to play, but we need an instrument and a teacher. Could you help him?"

"It would be my pleasure, *signora*. Bring him over and let me show him the instrument."

In the following weeks, Beppino went to Mr. Rossi's house whenever he could. The kind musician showed him the basics of the violin and let him practice while he was there. Each time Beppino came home chattering about what he had learned and begging to go back. After a dozen of these sessions, there was a knock on the Bassos' door. It was Mr. Rossi, asking for Teopista.

"Mrs. Pini, may I speak to you about Beppino?"

"Of course, *signore*. Is he becoming a bother? All he wants to do is go to your house, and I am afraid it is too much to ask of you. I am sorry."

"No, no. That's not it at all. Mrs. Pini, I believe your son has real talent. He is learning faster than I would have thought possible, and he gets better even when all he did was go home to sleep. I came here to suggest that you find him a real teacher. The man to go see is Louis Jacobs, in Atlantic Mine. I'm afraid Beppino has too much talent for someone like me to teach. He deserves better." Mr. Rossi was apologetic.

Teopista thought for a moment. Atlantic Mine was two and a half miles from South Range. By the time Beppino got home from school, Pista was working non-stop at the boarding house. How would she get him over to Atlantic Mine for a lesson, assuming Mr. Jacobs would take him and assuming she could find an instrument for Beppino to play?

"*Grazie,* Mr. Rossi. I am sure you're right about my son. I will just have to find a way."

"Mrs. Pini," said Mr. Rossi, "I would like to help. I will go with you to meet Mr. Jacobs, and if he agrees to teach Beppino, my wife is willing to walk him over to Atlantic Mine for his lessons. Beppino may borrow my violin until he gets one of his own. It will do me good to help a young prodigy like your son.

What do you think?"

"Mr. Rossi! This is the most wonderful offer, thank you. Yes, let's go meet this Mr. Jacobs."

Teopista was six months pregnant, and by the time she, Beppino, and Mr. Rossi had walked two and a half miles over the snow-packed streets to see Mr. Jacobs, she had to sit down. Mr. Jacobs was kind.

"To what do I owe the pleasure of this delegation?" he asked his visitors.

Mr. Rossi spoke better English than Teopista. "Sir, we want that you meet Giuseppe Pini. I believe this boy is musical— what do you call it?—very very good. He want to play violin."

Mr. Jacobs looked at the pale boy standing quietly next to his mother. "Hello, Giuseppe. So you like the violin?"

Beppino gave a shy nod. "Yes, sir."

"Well, you are smart. It is a beautiful instrument." Mr. Jacobs handed Beppino a violin. "Here, let me see what you can do."

Beppino squawked out a note and shook his head. "Sorry." He tried again, playing a few notes with increasing confidence.

"He has a gift," said Mr. Rossi, "but he need good teacher. Like you."

Teopista was agitated. She touched Mr. Rossi's arm. "You have to tell him we have no money," she said. "I will be able to pay only a very little bit." Mr. Rossi found the words to tell Louis Jacobs that Teopista's husband had left her. She and Beppino and his sister slept in a barn at night and Teopista worked in a boarding house.

Louis Jacobs sat back in his chair. "I'll tell you what. I will give Giuseppe lessons for three months at no charge. Then we will see. If he shows talent, we will discuss terms for continuing. If not, we will stop there. Okay?"

Teopista smiled from ear to ear. "Thank God for you, Mr. Jacobs. Three months, and then we see. Beppino, isn't this wonderful?"

Beppino looked up at Mr. Jacobs and gave a timid smile. "*Grazie,* thank you, sir."

Mr. Rossi loaned Giuseppe his violin, and every week for

the next three months he or his wife walked with Beppino to Atlantic Mine for a lesson with Louis Jacobs. The snow-packed streets gradually degenerated into ice and mud, slowing down their walk until it took over an hour each way. Beppino hardly noticed. He was in heaven. He came home from his lessons looking happier than Teopista had ever seen her quiet boy, and he practiced with a focus that seemed impossible for a six-year-old. "I had a feeling he was special," she told Mrs. Basso one day. "Music is his talent."

Beppino's tones were uneven at first, and some fairly awful screeches echoed through the boarding house, but increasingly he mastered the art of a light but confident bow stroke. He was hard on himself. When a practice session wasn't going well, Beppino would stamp his foot and walk away to sulk, though Teopista noticed he was always gentle with the instrument. Usually he picked it back up the same day, determined to do better.

The boarding house miners made fun of Giuseppe in the early days. They covered their ears and teased him. "That thing sounds like a sick monkey, kid. You're killing us, here." "Violins are for girls. Hey, maybe he's a girl!" But one day a quieter man named Mario spoke up. "Hey guys, lay off. Listen—the kid's not bad."

"Mario, is that a tear in your eye? I think it is! Mario's going all sentimental on us." One of the tougher miners elbowed the guy next to him. "Look at that. Mario's a girl, too!"

But Italians are no strangers to sentiment and the teasing didn't last. The beauty of the music and the intensity of the small boy catalyzed a shift in the boarding house. Mrs. Basso softened a little, and so did the miners. They could be a rough crowd but, for many, their toughness was more a response to circumstances than an innate quality. It wasn't just Mario who could be brought to tears by Beppino's music, especially when a man was particularly tired or missing home.

At the end of the three-month trial period, it was Louis Jacobs who made the trip to see Teopista. "Mrs. Pini," he said, "I have concluded that your son may be a prodigy. He has shown the depth of character needed to develop, he practices hard, and I would like to continue to teach him, if this is acceptable to you.

"But there is something else. He needs an instrument of his own, a better one than Mr. Rossi's. I can get one, but not for free. I will loan you the money if you can pay me back a little bit each week."

Teopista was hugely pregnant now and on the verge of giving birth, but she didn't hesitate. "*Sì,* Mr. Jacobs. Yes, and thank you! I will pay a little bit each week for my Beppino to have a violin. You are very kind." Pista had no idea where she'd get the money, but there was no question of saying no.

It was late June of 1916. Pista was having more and more trouble pulling herself up out of her bed on the hay. Her back hurt and her ankles were swollen beyond recognition. She was desperately uncomfortable, which she knew meant the time was near. In the middle of the night a few days later, she felt her water break. She lay in gritty silence for a while, not wanting to awaken her children as the pains advanced. But suddenly she realized that this labor was moving quickly.

"Iolanda," she nudged her sleeping daughter. "You have to help me. The baby is coming."

Iolanda shook herself awake. "Mama! What?"

"Go to the house and pour some hot water into a bucket. Bring it back, with some towels. Go quickly now."

Before she knew it, Teopista was trying to hold back a baby eager to be born. It felt like a long time Iolanda was gone, and when she returned, she found her mother bathed in sweat. "Okay, *cara,* are you ready?" Pista spoke in short bursts. "Aiiiieeee! The baby is coming. Take a warm, wet towel. Watch for the head."

Eleven-year-old Iolanda's eyes were like saucers. "Okay, Mama."

Pista groaned. "When the baby comes, hold the towel underneath."

"Yes, Mama."

"Now!" Teopista grimaced with the intense pain, and willed herself to push. She cried out as the head crowned, and with one more push, she felt the baby slide out. She had given birth in a barn. *Like the Mother Mary,* she thought.

"Okay, Iolanda, have you got the baby on the towel?"

"Yes, Mama." Iolanda looked terrified.

"Good girl," said Teopista. "Now, set down the baby, still on the towel. Be gentle. You see there is a cord attached to the baby?"

"*Sì.*"

"Go get Mrs. Basso. Tell her to come out here with a knife to cut that cord, okay *cara?* And run. Thank you."

Donata Basso was shocked. "Why didn't you come get me earlier? My God, I would have brought you inside and gotten the midwife!"

"There was no time," said Pista, "and you needed your rest. Anyway, Iolanda was a perfect assistant."

Donata placed the baby in Teopista's arms. "Congratulations," she said. "You have a son. You are a crazy woman, Teopista."

"I know, but what can I do? Welcome to the world, baby Alimando."

After Faustino Pini's disappearance in 1916, Teopista waited months before making contact with Francesco Rugani. She harbored uncertainty about Pini—would he or wouldn't he return? And she had a third child—not Pini's, not Cecco's, but Giuseppe Rugani's. Her cheeks flushed with shame as she imagined confessing this to Cecco. She was the mother of three children with three different fathers, all due to her irrepressible nature. Why would Francesco want anything to do with her? Pista nursed the baby Alimando, peeled potatoes for the miners, and made the best of her diminished life spent sleeping in a barn.

That autumn, on a Sunday afternoon, there was a knock on the Bassos' boarding house door. Every time a visitor came, Pista hoped and worried it would be Faustino Pini. Her husband's return would restore her respectability, get the family out of the barn, and give her a break from endless domestic labor. But if he did return, it was inevitable that there would be another explosion some day, for some reason. Both hope and worry were wasted, however, because it never was Pini at the door. This day it was the opposite of PIni: it was Francesco Rugani, asking to see Teopista.

She came running. "Cecco! Oh my God, it's you. I was afraid to contact you, but I wanted to so badly. Come in, have a grappa."

Francesco told Teopista that he, too, had been holding back. He knew Pini could show up any day, but he was dying to see her. "Pista, I couldn't stand being so close to you, with no contact. I had to come."

Teopista felt tears spring to her eyes. "Cecco, we have so much to talk about. But, before anything else, I have to tell you something. When I do, you may want nothing more to do with me."

Francesco leaned forward and looked her in the eye. "I know about the baby, Pista. Beppe wrote and told me. He asked me to look out for you and for baby Alimando. I was angry for a while, *sì*, but I got over it. It's okay, Pista."

Teopista cried for real now, recognizing the selflessness of both Rugani brothers. "You have no idea how worried I have been about this, Cecco. I thought I could never make things right, ever." Pista suddenly could not stop crying.

Cecco took her hands in his. "Pista, it's your nature. That's why we both love you, just like everyone else who meets you. But Pista, there is something I need to tell you in return. Beppe wrote me a very serious letter," said Cecco. "He wrote that I should not go back to Italy as we had planned. The war has made conditions so bad at home that the best thing for the family is for me to stay here, work, and send them money."

Teopista wiped her eyes and let this message sink in. Did this mean Cecco might never go home? What about her, and the children? She had never intended to stay in this rough mining town with the terrible winters. Staying indefinitely was not a prospect Pista could digest.

She and Cecco spent the rest of the visit on lighter topics. As he left, he promised to come back in a week. From that day forward, Francesco walked from Baltic to the Bassos' boarding house in South Range every Sunday, regardless of the weather, to spend the afternoon with Pista and the three children. He treated Iolanda, Beppino, and baby Allie with equal kindness, bringing the older children a piece of candy or a whistle he'd fashioned out of wood, bouncing the baby on his knee.

When the older children were out of earshot, he and Pista talked. They gave serious consideration to returning to Torcigliano Alto despite Beppe's warning. Cecco's salary as a trammer was miniscule, and Pista was working herself to exhaustion at the boarding house. Wouldn't it be better to be out in the Tuscan sunshine, helping the family? Cecco wrote home to Beppe, proposing that all five of them return.

Beppe's reply came immediately. "Don't do it, Cecco. We miss you terribly, but if you were here, we'd have to feed five more people, without benefit of the money you have been sending us. You have no idea how important that little bit is. Stay in America, Cecco, please, for the sake of the family."

The winter day that Cecco read this letter to Teopista, they sat in silence for a while. Pista was heartbroken, but ever practical. "Okay, then," she said. "We stay." She had been thinking this over for weeks now. "Cecco, if we are going to live here, we must do better for ourselves. The first step is to get married."

"What?" Cecco stared at the woman he adored, but didn't always understand. "Pista, what are you saying?"

Teopista had reached this decision with trepidation. She loved Cecco, more than she had ever loved Faustino Pini. But she was still married to Pini in the eyes of the church. It would be a sin to divorce, which she could not do because she didn't know where Pini was, and an even bigger sin to marry again without a divorce. But what if Pini never returned? She did not want to live as a single woman for the rest of her life, and she was too religious to live with Cecco without having married him. Teopista was a "pick and choose" kind of Catholic. She could live with herself for indulging in dalliances outside her marriage, but she would never set up housekeeping with a man she was not married to. There was no good solution, so she spent days worrying. By the time she said anything to Francesco, she had decided to take the risk.

"*Sì, mio amore,* I am sure. But you must be very sure, as well. If Pini returns, we will have a real problem. Even if he doesn't, we will be committing a sin, both of us."

"Pista, you know I am not overly concerned with the church. But Pini, yes, I am worried about him. If he comes back, he could kill us."

Francesco got up and looked out the window. "Okay, Pista, here's the thing. You are my first and only true love, and the mother of our son, Giuseppe. I love Iolanda and Allie just as much. I know for sure it is not right for you to live alone just because Pini is a son of a bitch. I would like nothing better than to be your husband, so yes, let's get married."

Romantic marriage proposals were not common for Italians in those days. Teopista's reply was simple: "*Bene,* that's settled." But her smile betrayed her emotions. "Cecco, thank you. I know this is not a good situation, and yet, I am so happy we will be together. You are a better man than I deserve."

She had already thought about their next step. "Now, we must go see Caesare Cappo. He has influence, and I intend to convince him to help us." For maximum effect, she had decided to bring baby Allie on the visit.

Cappo was known to love babies, so when they arrived at his office, she played this card first. "*Signore* Cappo, I'd like you to meet our son, Alimando," she said. "He loves to be tickled! Would you like to make him laugh?" She handed the baby to Cappo, whose face had already crinkled up into a smile.

Her next move was to flatter the powerful man. "*Signore,* everywhere I go I meet people who respect you. The Italians here would be in poor shape indeed without your influence." Cappo was playing with the baby, but Pista could tell she had his attention.

"Signore, Faustino Pini has been gone for a year now, and I believe he is never going to come back. As you can imagine, this leaves me in an insecure position as a single woman with three children. Francesco and I are friends from way back, and we have made a decision. We would like to be married. We hope you will give us your blessing."

"Of course, and congratulations to you both," said Cappo.

That was the easy part. "*Grazie mille,* Signore Cappo," said Teopista, as she willed baby Allie to continue to smile and coo in Cappo's lap. "You are most kind. Would you now entertain another question? You know I have been living in the Bassos' barn, with all three of my children. Francesco lives in a boarding house. We need a better situation, and we need to earn money to send back to our families at home. They are suffering, as are all our loved ones during this terrible war. Signore, I wonder if you have any suggestion for how we might better our lives. As you know, we are willing to work hard."

Cappo regarded them. Allie played his part perfectly, making an adorable little noise that drew an additional tickle from their benefactor. "Here is what I can offer you," he said. "The Vanni family doesn't want to run their boarding house in Baltic any more. Signore Andreini owns it, and I think he would help you buy it, if you pay him back over time and agree to provide space for the men we send over to you. You will get out of the barn, and earn some money of your own. How about that?"

"We'll do it," said Teopista, without even consulting Cecco. "*Grazie,* Signore Cappo!"

Cecco looked a little overwhelmed, but he mustered a thank you as they shook Cappo's hand and headed back out on the street with the baby.

Caesare Cappo, like Dominick Zana, was a political creature. The more favors he granted to the local Italian community, the more influence he garnered. He may not have known, in 1917, exactly how he would make use of his influence over Francesco Rugani and his wife, but it never hurt to create a possibility for the future.

Teopista's next step was to visit Zana, asking him to sponsor

Francesco Rugani's petition for American citizenship. In 1917, when a man became a naturalized United States citizen, his wife and children automatically earned citizenship as well. In a matter of weeks, Cecco and Pista submitted their petition for citizenship, got married, and began running a boarding house for Italian miners in Baltic, Michigan. Cecco still went to work in the mine every day, and Teopista still labored incessantly to keep the boarding house running, but they had taken a step up economically, and they were able to send a little more money back home.

The boarding house came with enough extra property that Francesco could create a miniature farm. They needed the food he raised, and the work of a farmer reminded him of home. He grew a vegetable garden, kept chickens for eggs, and raised a milking cow and a pig. He became known for his *delizioso prosciutto,* which the boarders loved. When word got out to the neighbors, Pista began receiving visitors bearing gifts they hoped to exchange for just *un po,* just a little bit, *per favore,* of Francesco's famous *prosciutto? Grazie mille,* thank you, Pista!

The Rugani's boarding house was fun, as was to be expected in an establishment run by Teopista. Miners off-shift would gather in the big kitchen to drink wine, share stories, and play cards. At any hour a man could join in a game of *briscola,* testing his wits with tricks and trumps. On Saturday nights it was here that neighbors gathered for a party, with music, dancing, and ample food and drink. Although Pista and Cecco were constantly tired, they were happy. Teopista grew round from the neighbors' gifts of cake and treats, and then she grew even rounder with a new pregnancy. They named the baby Rosina.

Conditions in America during the First World War were far better than in Europe, but still awful. More than 300,000 American soldiers came home in coffins or on stretchers. And then, just as the war was finally coming to an end in 1918, a massive flu epidemic swept the globe.

"Cecco, Pista, listen to this!" A neighbor came over in October with newspaper in hand. "Influenza has reached the Copper Country. This story says that a medical team pumped a handcar over the railroad tracks for twenty miles to find a tiny log cabin in the woods, full of people all sweating with 104-degree fevers." Teopista crossed herself and prayed the sickness would not come to their house or to their friends. She had heard that doctors now believed diseases were passed through germs, so in between feedings of Rosina, she redoubled her efforts to keep the house meticulously clean. It was exhausting, and teenaged Iolanda was an increasingly sullen and unwilling helper. Before the epidemic ended, an estimated 675,000 Americans, incredibly, had died of the flu. Whether due to her prayers or her scrubbing, Teopista managed to keep the boarding house illness-free, but work and worry took their toll.

Pista's sister Rosina, for whom the baby was named, came from Loppeglia to help out. She was a stunning beauty who received three marriage proposals within two months. "Sorry, Pista," she said. "Saturday nights here are fun, but the rest of the time it's just work, work, work. I'm going to get married." As quickly as Rosina had arrived, she was gone.

Three more years and a fifth baby later, relief finally appeared. Dominick Zana and his associates had a use for the Ruganis, and his proposal would release them from boarding house drudgery.

"Francesco and Teopista, *buon giorno,*" said Zana. He wore a meticulously tailored suit, and the hand he extended bore a chunky gold ring. "How would you like to run your own grocery store?"

Teopista was, for once, caught off-guard. "*Che?* What are you proposing, *signore?*"

"You know the store on Trimountain Avenue in South Range? Giulio and Ralph, who run the place, are moving away. Andreini and I will help you get started financially, and believe, me, there is money to be made in the grocery business. This is a great opportunity for you."

What Zana did not tell Cecco and Pista was that the money he referenced would not come from sales of flour and eggs, but from traincars loaded with grapes and corn sugar. Prohibition had created an opportunity for power brokers like Zana to run a widespread bootlegging operation. They needed grocers to provide the ingredients, and the one store in South Range run by Italians was their source. The Ruganis would make a modest profit, but Zana's tailored suits and chunky gold rings were financed through the end product, bootleg liquor sold in blind pigs, underground bars where it was an open secret that a man in need of a drink would be served.

What Zana was offering Cecco and Pista was a place on the ladder of Italian power, not near the top, but several steps up from the tedious boarding house.

"We'll take it," said Pista. Cecco swallowed and offered his hand to Zana to shake on the deal.

The move paid off. Francesco was out from the underground, and Teopista no longer had to clean and cook all day long. The grocery business required long hours, but the work was much easier and the money better. Their letters home to Beppe and the family contained larger gifts and a brighter tone. "Beppe, you wouldn't believe it. We run a store now."

What Francesco did not tell his brother was that he had become involved with a criminal element. He lived in fear of what could happen if he failed to meet his obligations as a supplier. It was Teopista who was certain they were doing the right thing. "Cecco, would you rather do this, or go back underground in the mine? Look how much better our lives are now. We've come up in the world."

Cecco nodded. "You are right, Pista. It's just that some of these guys are really tough. God forbid we get them angry." Cecco had been making deliveries to obscure locations all over the Copper Country, where a network of Italians operated stills in the woods and moved their product under cover of darkness, greasing palms to ensure a tip-off when the feds were coming. The stakes were high, and testosterone flowed as freely as the booze. Franscesco thought wistfully of the old days out in the Tuscan sunshine, pruning olive trees and joking with his brothers. He sighed. *As Teopista likes to say, we do what we must do, not what we want to do.*

Family life at home was a great consolation. As foreseen by Mr. Rossi and Louis Jacobs, Beppino had become a virtuoso violinist, and the other children were lively. Saturday night celebrations moved from the boarding house to the Rugani apartment above the store, where they rolled back the rug and half of South Range came to dance and sing and tell tales until all hours. It was the one time in the week when the whole family, including nervous Cecco, let loose and had fun.

One Sunday, after a raucous Saturday night, Beppino woke up feeling poorly. "Mama, I am sick again," he told Pista. Beppino had not outgrown his delicate constitution, and he commonly grew overtired, spending several days in bed. Pista drew the blinds to help her son rest, and prepared her signature chicken soup. Beppino gave her a sad smile. "*Grazie*, Mama, but I am not hungry. Maybe later. Mama, I am so tired of being sick. Why does this always happen to me?"

"It is because you have a gift, *caro*," said Teopista. "God gave you a sensitive nature so you could make music like an angel." Beppino took comfort in her words, but later in the day he was not better, nor was he able to eat the next day.

"Cecco, help!" On Wednesday, Teopista ran downstairs to her husband in an uncharacteristic panic. "Beppino's illness is much, much worse. He needs to go to the hospital in Trimountain, now!"

"Okay, Pista, let's think. I have to make a delivery to Seeberville and it can't wait. Alimando will have to drive."

"But Allie is only eight years old! He can't even reach the pedals on the truck. Can't you make the delivery later, please, Cecco?"

"Pista, you know I cannot. I must fill this order or Zana will kill me. I have shown Alimando how to drive. I'll set up the truck so he can operate it."

Francesco turned the front seat of the old Rio truck around 180 degrees and angled the back so that Allie could reach the pedals with his feet and still see out the windshield. Teopista and Francesco carried their gravely ill son to the truck and laid him down. Teopista climbed in next to Beppino and caressed his fever-soaked forehead. "Hang on, *caro*. We're getting you to the doctor."

"Now, Allie," said Cecco, "remember when I showed you the clutch and the gas? Do what I taught you, and take your brother to the Trimountain Hospital. It's two miles and you won't have to stop once you get going. I'll help you make the first turn. I know you can do this, son."

Allie Rugani swallowed. "Yes, Pa." After a couple of lurching false starts, he got the truck rolling. Francesco jogged alongside and reached in to turn the wheel onto the road to Trimountain. He straightened the truck and encouraged his son as he let go. "Good boy, Allie. You can do this."

With his brother barely conscious in the back of the truck, Alimando gripped the wheel and pressed on the gas. The truck jumped. It was a straight shot to Trimountain, but once he got there, he had to make one more turn to reach the hospital. Allie mumbled a prayer and turned the wheel. He saw he was going too fast, so he put on the brake and the truck stalled. Allie couldn't get it started again. "Mama, I can't do it!"

Teopista got out and ran faster than her ample body should have allowed. She was breathing so hard when she reached the hospital that she could barely speak. "Help us, please!" she said. "My son! Down there, in truck, very sick!"

Pista gripped her rosary as Beppino was taken to an examination room. Her delicate boy was fifteen years old. He had played concerts in every venue in the area, to roars of appreciation from audiences. Most recently, Mr. Jacobs had secured an invitation for Giuseppe to play with a symphony orchestra from New York. Pista and Cecco were in awe of their son.

The doctor emerged, and Pista could tell by the expression on his face that the news was bad. "I'm afraid Giuseppe's appendix burst, and he has a condition called peritonitis." Pista did not understand, and she looked at Allie for help.

"What is peri—perito—what did you say, sir?" asked Allie.

"It is a very serious infection," said the doctor. "I am sorry, but his chances are not good. There is no treatment other than drainage tubes, and his body may not be strong enough to fight this off."

This was a message Teopista understood. "Doctor, our boy *will* live. We stay with him and pray to God to make him strong."

Pista did not sleep for three days. She sat by Beppino's side and prayed, as her son moaned and his breathing grew increasingly labored. "Beppino, my love, be strong. Fight this off and come back to your family and your music. I love you more than life itself." She would not allow herself to consider the possibility of losing him, but on the fourth day, Giuseppe's body gave up its struggle. Her gifted, delicate, beloved son was gone.

Teopista was devastated. She sat in a daze in the apartment over the store, as people came from all over bringing food and condolences. The funeral mass at Holy Family Church was a blur, with Giuseppe laid out in an open casket and the church overflowing with mourners. Hundreds of people had heard Beppino play, and they knew he was about to perform with a real symphony from New York. They had been as proud of their local boy as if they had personally had a hand in his success. With his death, they lost this source of pride, and lost, too, their hopes for a grander life, something that transcended the daily grind.

Teopista's loss included these same things and so much more: her first-born son, her sensitive boy with the rare gift for music. He was her hope for the future and her tie to the past, a connection to her home in Italy, and to one of the happiest times of her life, living in Torcigliano Alto with the Ruganis. As the weeks passed, Pista's grief did not abate. Unable to sleep, she took to walking the streets of South Range in the middle of the night, ending up at the cemetery where Beppino was buried. In the winter, she placed blankets over his grave to keep him warm. During the day she was a husk of her former self.

Eight-year-old Alimando was devastated, too, but while

Teopista grieved openly, Allie bottled up his pain. No one had blamed him for Beppino's death, but he was tormented by the thought that if he had not stalled the truck, maybe Beppino wouldn't have died. As his mother's impenetrable grief dragged on, Allie grew sure that she didn't love him any more, because his presence seemed to mean nothing to her. A protective shell quietly grew around Allie's heart.

Francesco was at a loss. He had no idea how to help his wife, and he had to run the store without her help. Not knowing what else to do, Cecco turned to Iolanda. At eighteen years old, she was competent to help with ordering and managing the business, and unlike her parents, Iolanda spoke fluent English. She was worried enough about her mother not to complain more than a little about the work, and she rose to the occasion. She was less happy about taking care of the younger three children, but this, too, had to be done. If there had been any doubt that Teopista was the head of the family, those doubts vanished in the months she was incapacitated.

"Pista, *amore,* please!" The Copper Country winter had dragged on and on, with no sign of life from Teopista. Six months had passed since Beppino's death, and Cecco was desperate to have his wife back. "We need you." No response.

"Okay, then, I am going for help." Francesco put on his one good suit, and trudged down the slushy road to the church.

"Father Mario, it's Teopista. She is half-crazy with grief, even after all this time. She walks the streets at night and sits blankly all day. I don't know what to do. Help us, please."

The priest walked back to the store with Francesco and climbed the stairs to the apartment where Pista sat staring out the window.

"My daughter," he said, "I have come to pray with you." As he offered the Hail Mary and the Our Father, Teopista began to move her lips with his words. When they were done, she met the priest's gaze. Her eyes were deep pools of suffering but she did not look away.

"*Signora,* you can be certain that your Beppino is in heaven. He does not suffer. You know, too, that God has given you strength to withstand every hardship, even this one. *Signora,* it is time to return to your family. Francesco, Iolanda, Alimando, Rosina, and Gena, they need you. Return to this world. It is time."

Grazie a Dio, it worked. Teopista rose from her stupor and took up her place in the family. Relief flooded out the apartment windows, down the stairs and throughout the store. Not one hundred percent and not all at once, but Pista was back.

Alimando was not back, but no one noticed. He went to school, progressing as expected. He and two boys from the more powerful Italian families became The Three Musketeers, specializing in annoying people and telling stories that grew more dramatic with each new version. Teopista became accustomed to one or another South Range neighbor coming to the store in the afternoon, not to buy milk but to take her aside.

"Pista, can you do something about Allie? He and his gang came to the Chinese laundry and said they would pee on our windows if we didn't give them a penny." Another day it was Mrs. Valentino. "Pista, my husband is too embarrassed to talk to you himself, so I'm here. Your son tipped over our outhouse, door-side down, while my husband was in it! You must stop him."

Teopista was sympathetic, but she had little influence over Alimando. He had grown independent and moody since Beppino's death, and she had been too broken to pay much attention. Now he was running wild with his friends, and she didn't even understand their English, let alone know how to moderate their behavior. The other mothers were no help. Their boys could do no wrong in their eyes, and Pista could see that they were actually proud of their tough sons. She scolded Allie about Old Man Valentino's outhouse, but didn't press the point.

At Painesdale High School, Alimando ate his lunch "Italian

style," meaning that Teopista filled his Thermos with red wine instead of milk. When his teacher told the principal she had a student drinking wine at lunch, the principal paid a visit to Pista at the store.

"Mrs. Rugani," she said, "you cannot be sending your son to school with wine. Please give him milk, for his health."

Teopista regarded her visitor. "You know, Mrs. Jeffers," she said, "a lotta time the sickness is passed on with sour milk. Milk is no good for my son to be healthy. The wine has no disease, and it makes a nice red blood for my boy." Mrs. Jeffers was not swayed by this argument, but the women agreed to a compromise: water.

Allie listened to this conversation and grew quietly angry. Water! Water was not a real drink. Mrs. Jeffers didn't like Italians, he was sure, a conclusion that later hardened into certainty.

Alimando was a very good athlete. Sports were a way to channel his pent-up anger, grief, and self-recrimination. He made the district all-star basketball team. However, when the all-stars were recognized on stage at school, Allie was over-looked. Only an English boy, who was an alternate and not as good as Allie, was recognized. Alimando seethed.

The coach took him aside. "Allie," he said, "you have talent and you know it. Let's get you a basketball scholarship for college. I'll help you."

Allie was skeptical. "Ahh, I don't know, coach. I figure I'll stay here and help out with the store."

"Come on, Allie, you can do better. Let's give it a try."

In the spring of 1934, an envelope arrived in the mail from Chicago. "Dear Alimando, We are pleased to inform you that you have been accepted to Northwestern University on a full basketball scholarship. Congratulations!"

For a full week, Allie told no one about the letter. After failing to save his brother's life ten years before, Allie had compensated by refusing to fail at anything, ever again. He studied until his brain felt as if it would explode, he played sports with a burning intensity, and he did whatever his parents expected or he guessed they might expect. What would they want him to do now? As a teenager, he had become indispensable to his father in the store. But perhaps his parents would want him to better himself, and make the family proud by going to college.

Alimando could not admit to himself that he was afraid of failing as a college student, but he must have been, or else he would have sat down with Teopista and Francesco and discussed the letter. Instead, he brooded alone until he had reached a decision. The family needs me here, he told himself. *I am the only son. It is my job to run the store.* Allie went out behind the house and quietly burned the letter. *Damn it!* He clenched his jaw and strode back into the store. Pista and Cecco never knew their son was offered a scholarship to go to college.

Alimando had been working for his father since he was twelve years old. When he became strong enough to lift heavy objects, Francesco began taking him out on deliveries. During the day they brought groceries to housewives who invited them in for coffee. Most families in the Copper Country in the 1920s did not have a car, so a visit from the grocery store men was an event. Chatting up these customers was as important to the business as the food itself. The more fun a woman had, the more certain she was to renew her order.

In reponse to Prohibition, many families ordered quantities of grapes in order to make their own wine, legal up to 200 gallons per year. Business was so brisk that Francesco asked Allie to recruit his friends to help with deliveries. The boys were glad to help out, until they discovered how little the frugal store owner paid them for their trouble. "That old man is tighter than the bark on a tree," they grumbled. But they came back the next week to help again. Any job at all was better than none.

Local Italian families who took up wine-making made the most of Prohibition. Even the most celebratory family was unlikely to need 200 gallons for personal consumption, so they kept the good virgin wine for themselves, and then added sugar and water to the mash to create a lower-quality product. Called *picciolo,* this beverage was quietly sold to unsuspecting non-Italians as table wine. From there, the remaining mash was squeezed and distilled into grappa, nearly 100% pure alcohol, and still there was one more use for the leftovers. Dried-up mash could be spread over the gardens as fertilizer. This cascade of products originated with the California grapes that Francesco ordered and Alimando and his friends delivered.

At night the work took on a decidedly different character. Francesco started up the truck at midnight, to deliver hundred-pound bags of corn sugar to the homes of area bootleggers. Allie would sling a huge bag over his shoulder and carry it to the top floor of the house, where he poured the granules through a hole between two studs. The space was lined with copper, allowing a clean column of sugar to flow all the way down to the basement, where the distiller extracted it by raising a small metal door. Rugani's Market sold corn sugar in one-ton lots, which meant twenty bags had to be hauled up the stairs. Allie was exhausted when it was time for basketball practice the next day, but his muscles were rock-hard.

"Cecco," Teopista approached her husband one day. "I am worried about these night-time deliveries. It's dangerous for Alimando, and he is falling asleep in class the next day. What is he learning? To be above the law? I don't like it."

"I know," said Cecco. "But I must make these deliveries, and I cannot do it without his help. Our business depends on this money, Pista."

She shook her head. "I still no like it."

One day a sheriff's deputy stopped by the store and whispered in Francesco's ear. "The feds are coming. Do what you need to do." That afternoon Allie watched as a puffed-up stranger strolled into the store and his father transformed into a dumb Italian immigrant, selling dried olives and codfish.

"May I help you, *signore?*" asked Francesco, with a smile. "Would you like some very good olives?"

"I ain't here to talk about olives, and you know it," said the stranger. "I've seen your orders. Why are you buying corn sugar by the traincar load?"

"Well, you know," said Francesco, "I sell the sugar to many people. The Finns around here, they do a lot of baking."

The man snorted through his big red nose. "Right, okay. You show me your route today, and we'll see who these 'bakers' might be. If they're making booze, I'll be able to smell it."

"No problem, *signore*," said Francesco. "My son will show you. Alimando, take this man out in the truck and show him our customers."

"Yes, Pa," said Allie. This part of the job was fun, and he knew what to do. With the fed in tow, he pulled up at the home of a sugar customer. "I don't know much about this man, sir," Allie said, "but I see them in church all the time. Very religious. I'm sure they wouldn't be involved in anything illegal."

The fed got out of the truck, sniffed around with his red nose, and agreed. "There's nothing going on here."

Two houses down, Allie stopped the truck again. "These people buy groceries, but I don't see them in church. Can't say what you might find here." The fed got out of the truck and caught a whiff of alcohol. He knocked on the door. A personable, friendly, and innocent Englishman greeted him. "Hello! Please come in, sir. You are welcome to look at anything you like." The fed searched the house and cursed under his breath as he left empty-handed.

The man was a "Cousin Jack," an Englishman in collusion with his Italian neighbor down the street. In exchange for a steady supply of product, Cousin Jacks would allow underground vent pipes to emerge in their yards. The distillery would be at one home, while the odor emanated from another. Everyone was happy, except the red-nosed fed.

After Prohibition ended in 1933, Rugani's Market continued to make a profit on alcohol-related sales. Blind pigs, as the illegal bars were called, stayed open, enjoying tax-free revenue. In addition, the area's logging camps began placing large orders for beer. It was not uncommon for Alimando to deliver fifty cases of beer to a camp on a Saturday morning, and return that same evening to pick up all fifty cases, empty.

While the bootleggers were Italian, the loggers were mostly Finnish. They were big, muscular, fearless guys who spent their days felling massive virgin pines and running them down rivers. Allie was strong and tough, but next to these men he felt shrimpy, which he did not enjoy, so he quietly took up boxing. One winter afternoon he pulled up at a local home to make a delivery. He was chatting with the customer when she looked out the window and said, "Allie! A bunch of huge guys are carrying your truck off the road!"

Alimando ripped off his shirt and ran outside in his bib underwear top. He chose the biggest of the Finns and cold-cocked him. One punch and the guy was on his back in the snow.

"Anyone else want to join him?" he said to the shocked Finns. "If not, you will move that truck back where you found it. Dust the snow off, too."

Word got around that Allie Rugani was crazy, and the truck incident did not recur. Even so, Allie wanted another layer of protection, so he started carrying a pistol. The logging camps paid in cash and by the end of a day's deliveries he had a sizeable amount of money in a wallet chained to his belt. His last stop was Giacolletto's Bar, to pick up Mrs. Giacolletto's grocery order. Allie was chatting with Joe Giacolletto at the bar when a logger stepped up behind him and snatched the wallet with one hand and the pistol with the other. The wallet was attached to Allie, so the guy couldn't get away. Instead, he turned to the room and said, "Rugani's had a good day, so he's gonna buy everyone in here a drink."

"Tell you what," said Allie. "You put my pistol up on the bar. I'll unhook the wallet and we'll leave that here, too, with Joe. Then you and me, we'll step outside. One of us will walk back in here, and the other one will buy everyone that drink."

The beefy logger didn't want to admit he'd been had, so he put the pistol and the wallet on the bar, and swaggered outside after Allie.

It was Allie who strolled back in. "It's gonna take our friend a minute to make good on that drink," he told the customers. "He'll have to wake up first."

Allie had spent years watching his father live in fear of the Italian families higher up on the ladder of power. He grew to hate those people, whose sons had taunted him at school. "Your family is nothing, Rugani." Even the boys he hung around with, who acted friendly most of the time, he was sure were looking down on him behind his back. His closest friends were from the Lucchesi, Basso, Santori, and Andreini families, who had been a cut above the *contadini* back in Italy and brought their higher status with them to America. Alimando's father put up with his position in the second-tier, spouting that damnable phrase, "We do what we must do, not what we want to do." Allie hated that saying almost as much as he hated the possibility of being inferior. He loved his father and showed him respect but he wished Francesco were not so passive.

Stories of Alimando's bravado filtered back to Teopista at the store. Allie never said a word, but some customer would say, "Pista, that son of yours is something else! Was he even sore this morning?" When she asked him, Alimando said, "Ah, that was nothing. A guy tried to steal from me and I stopped him. That's all."

"Allie," Pista said one afternoon, "I worry you are working too hard. Don't you want to go on dates, go out with a girl?"

"Ma, that's none of your business."

"*Sì*, is my business. You spend all your time working, you get in fights, you need a girl. Someone to balance you, make you happy." Teopista grinned at her scowling son. "What about that Basso girl, Rosa? She very pretty, no? I will talk to her mother."

"Ma, no! Leave it alone, really, okay?"

Allie had, here and there, taken girls out on dates. Sometimes it was the sister of a friend, or a girl someone else set him up with for a double date. When the girl was from one of those higher-up families, though, she always ended up getting serious with someone else. Could have been coincidence, but Allie didn't think so. A familiar anger rose in his chest, and he slammed the wall. *They can all go to hell!* He knew the store needed those families for business purposes, so he held his head up and continued to be friends with the boys. But inside, he seethed.

One of the store's customers was a Finnish family named Harju. Allie delivered groceries to their farm in Mill Mine

Junction, where he was often received by Milma, an unmarried daughter around his age. Milma had been the studious, shy type of girl Allie never spoke to in high school. He hadn't known what to say to such a smart girl, nor did he want to risk sounding stupid. Over time, however, he began to look forward to his visits to the Harju farm, and Milma began to be home every time he appeared.

Finns never received a visitor without offering coffee and a bit of "bakery." Milma made an excellent *nissu,* Finnish coffee cake, and she smiled when Allie wolfed it down and told her how wonderful it was.

"Would you like some more, then?" she asked him.

"Well, since you asked, sure I would."

Milma had gone to Marquette Normal School and earned a bachelor's degree, one of just a few women in her class to do so. Now she taught a classroom of ten-year-olds in the local school. One Saturday she risked telling Allie a story about one of her boys, and he laughed so hard that she followed with another. Pretty soon she was surprised to find it easy to talk to this tough Italian grocery guy. For his part, Allie was intimidated by Milma's educational prowess, but telling stories, now *that* he could do. When she hung on every word, he felt a warm glow inside.

Their romance developed slowly. Perhaps it didn't occur to either of them that the other was marriage material. Milma surely would have planned to marry a college graduate, and Allie would find himself a local girl who could help out in the store. But when Milma made the choice to come back home to the farm after college, her pool of college-educated bachelors shrank to near zero. And, too, she had a bit of a contrarian streak. This emotional, charismatic Italian attracted her. He had a dark side she didn't understand, so much more interesting than the usual fare.

For his part, Allie liked how calm and clear-headed Milma was. She was smart, and she listened to him so completely. Who in his life did that? There was something else in her, too. She was determined. She had moved one hundred miles away to

Marquette to go to college, and now she presided over a class-room of forty children without ever seeming flustered. She was a rock, he thought, and an attractive one at that. But would someone like her consider going out with him? Not possible. He wasn't the right kind of people, and Allie hated to fail. For two full years he didn't do more than eat cake and tell stories at the Harju's kitchen table on delivery day.

Milma went out on dates with suitable men. One of them began to court her rather seriously and she thought perhaps she should marry him. At night, though, she dreamed of Allie Rugani. *Oh my God,* she thought. *Is it possible I'm in love with the Italian grocer? The Catholic Italian grocer??*

Once she admitted it to herself, there was no turning back for Milma. She took extra care with her hair and clothes on Saturday. She baked a perfect *pannukakku,* an eggy Finnish pancake, served with sauce from raspberries picked on the farm, and she laughed more than usual at Alimando's stories. As he was getting ready to leave, she said, "Allie, I don't think you've ever had a tour of our farm. Would you like to see it?"

Her mother looked sharply at her daughter. Being a reserved Finn, Teresia Harju didn't say anything in the moment, but that evening she spoke to her husband in private. "Oskar, I think Milma is sweet on that Italian grocery man."

"Come on, that's impossible." Oskar stared at his wife. "Teresia, if this is true, you must stop it. Our daughter did not go to college just to end up with a grocery man." He didn't need to mention the Italian and Catholic parts.

"I don't know what I can do with our willful daughter, Oskar, but I'll try."

The following week Milma had again dressed up in antici-pation of Allie's visit, when Teresia took her aside."Milma, I want you to come with me to visit the Kestis next door. Mrs. Kesti hasn't been well. We can bring her those nice cookies you baked."

"But that's when the groceries are coming, Mother, and I baked the cookies for Mr. Rugani. I must be here to take the order."

"Your sister Minda can receive the groceries, Milma. You will come with me, please."

On the way home from the Kesti farm, Teresia spoke her mind. "Milma, I am not blind. You do know that Allie Rugani is completely unsuitable, don't you? You are bettering yourself, as everyone in our family is meant to do. An uneducated grocer will drag you down. And Milma, a Catholic! The wine! Did we raise you Apostolic for nothing? You must put him out of your mind." Teresia softened a little. "I know it's hard to let go of an infatuation, but that's all it is. You can do better. What about that English man who was so interested not long ago?"

"The English man was dull, Mother," said Milma. "I know you want me to choose someone like him, but all I could see as I looked into the future was a life of predictability. Housework, children, meat and potatoes, Methodist church." She shook her head. "I'd rather be an old maid teacher for the rest of my life."

Milma did not talk back to her mother about Allie Rugani, but Teresia's approach backfired. Missing her weekly flirtation, on top of being told what to do, made Milma angry. She decided she would pursue Allie Rugani, consequences be damned.

Milma was twenty-five years old in 1939, and her teaching day ended in mid-afternoon. The following Monday when she left school, she walked over to the Rugani Market. Alimando was out on deliveries, so she left him a note. "Dear Alimando, I came by to see you. I will come again tomorrow, and hope you are here. Sincerely, Milma Harju."

Teopista had time to contemplate this note before her son returned. Alimando and a Finnish girl? Interesting! Pista wouldn't have predicted it, but the girl could be a good influence on her volatile son. Certainly it was good to have more education in the family.

When Allie read the note, he turned his head, but not before Teopista saw him blush. She teased him. "Got a girl, eh Allie? That Milma is a pretty one, too."

"Ma, it's nothing. She probably just forgot something in her grocery order." Allie banged the store's front door behind him and went straight to his friend Geno Lucchesi. Geno was dating an English girl from Wisconsin who had been to college and came to the Copper Country to work for the Stella Cheese Company.

"Geno! Talk to me! You're going out with a girl who isn't Italian. What do you think about me and a Finn?"

"Allie, you gotta try it. These girls aren't all bossy like the Italians. Is she, you know, va-va-voom?" Geno mimicked big boobs and pumped his eyebrows.

Both boys laughed. "Oh yeah," said Allie. "She's ample. And smart, and pretty."

"So, what more do you need? You've got her in your lap already." Geno elbowed Allie and leered at him.

Alimando still thought it was possible Milma just wanted some eggs, and he armored himself against disappointment, but he also made a point of being in the store the next day after school.

She came in looking beautiful. She looked more shy than usual as she handed him a plate of cookies. "These are for you. I didn't get to give them to you on Saturday."

She's interested. Allie was scared to death, but he took the risk. "Milma, would you like to go to the movies with me this weekend?"

So it was that, in defiance of her parents, Milma went out on a date with Allie Rugani. Three weeks later they were engaged. The Harjus were so upset they refused to attend the wedding and they pulled their business from the Rugani Market. The Finns in those days were sure that the Italians were all bootleggers and gangsters, while the Italians said, "Those Finns all got lice. They sleep with their cows." Allie and Milma didn't care.

The honeymoon was not all that a girl ever dreamed of. Allie told Milma they would be driving to Ohio to visit his sister Iolanda—who did not approve of their marriage.

"So I suppose she's pregnant," Iolanda said to Allie. "When's the baby due?"

"Iolanda," said Allie, "you apologize to my wife, who is absolutely not pregnant!" Allie wouldn't take a hand to his sister, but he wanted to. Instead of apologizing, Iolanda piled on by asking the newlyweds to drive her son back to the Copper Country with them to visit his relatives. Milma learned that Alimando was a lot tougher on local thugs than he was on his sister, to whom he could not say no. This was not the charismatic man she'd found so attractive. Her honeymoon concluded with a long drive punctuated by awkward attempts to talk to the sullen teenage boy in the back seat.

Back at home, the Harjus continued to be hostile toward the Ruganis. The Ruganis took a more passive-aggressive approach. "Milma's nice enough," Rose and Gena said to Allie, "but, you know, she's a *filandra*—a Finn," who would never measure up to Italian standards. Francesco Rugani wasn't sure what to think. He was courteous to all his customers and dealt with everyone fairly, but Milma as a wife to Alimando? She was so, well, foreign.

Teopista, as ever, was clear. "Milma is a person of learning," she said. "She is a good person. Good for our boy, good for our family. We welcome her. We must *all* welcome her." She glared at her critical daughters, who didn't meet her gaze.

Once she survived her honeymoon, Milma began to enjoy marriage. She escaped her parents, moved out of the Mill Mine Junction farmhouse, and set up housekeeping in a small home next door to the store in South Range. For the first time in her life she could walk to shops, and she held her head high as she nodded and smiled to the Italian matrons who were watching her. Her policy was to be nice to everyone. They could try to take her down, but for what? She would give them no reason.

Milma was not pregnant on her wedding day in May 1939, but a month later she suspected she might be. It happened so fast that she and Allie hadn't yet even spoken of children. As the hot summer progressed, Milma began to recognize signs of change in her body. In mid-August she grew sure.

"Allie, are you ready for a surprise? I'm pregnant."

Milma did not get the reaction she expected. Alimando stared at her. "You're joking, right?"

"No, I'm quite sure. We've been having fun!" Milma teased her husband, but it didn't change his mood.

"Milma, this is so soon. I thought you would be teaching this year."

"Allie, no. I would not have been teaching in any case. Married teachers are prohibited in our district. Remember, I told you this?"

Allie hadn't believed her, but in any case the point was moot with Milma pregnant. "Gosh, I'm going to have to get used to this whole thing. It's great, of course, but it's just so soon. I'm going out for a walk." He let the screen door bang behind him.

Milma suddenly felt deeply lonely. Her parents had written her off since she married the Italian grocer, and now her husband had reacted badly to news that should have been joyful. Come September, she would have no classroom full of spirited children to engage her mind. Her eyes filling, she cut herself a slice of *nissu* and sat at the table across from no one.

The early Copper Country fall gave way to cold and snow. Milma had always been philosophical about winter in the Upper Peninsula. Finns call it *sisu,* a quality of perseverance and spirit in the face of adversity that has no direct translation into English. This year, for the first time in her life, Milma found she did not have a supply of *sisu* at the ready.

On Saturday nights she and Allie were expected to appear at his parents' apartment next door for food, wine, and music. Teopista was the big, warm, emotional heart of the gathering, and always kind to Milma. Francesco was quieter yet also welcoming. Around the edges, however, Milma felt like a visitor from another planet. The Italians were noisy and gossipy, and their stories could be laced with little digs at one another. A loud argument would arise, and then subside as if nothing had happened. Sitting on the sidelines with her pregnant belly, Milma waited until Allie was ready to take her home.

Alimando grew to accept his wife's pregnancy but he never

lost his anxiety. During the week, he worked long hours at the store, shared a glass of grappa with his buddies, and often came home after Milma had climbed into bed. The time was flying. If only pregnancy took years rather than months! For Milma, of course, the problem was the reverse. Her days crawled.

They limped through, with no choice to do otherwise, and on March 23, 1940, Milma gave birth to a son. With this event, the world shifted. Milma exhaled with relief. Alimando puffed up and poured toasts for everyone in sight. The Harjus stopped being angry, and Teopista glowed. A baby! This boy would carry on the family name. He would be the one who succeeded in America. All was forgiven. Frank Charles Rugani was here.

Milma was no longer lonely. To the contrary, sometimes she wished the grandmothers would tone down their enthusiasm. Teresia called every day, hinting how nice it would be to see the baby. Several times a week, Milma felt obliged to drive out to the farm, where her mother cooed at the baby and plied Milma with bakery.

"Mother, how am I going to lose my baby weight?"

"You worry too much, Milma. Have another slice of cake."

On the Rugani side, Teopista didn't bother with a time-wasting phone call. She dropped in whenever she felt like it, scooping up her grandson and nuzzling him with a toothy smile. "Come for dinner tonight," she told her daughter-in-law. Pista liked nothing better than to preside over a family table. "More, eat more!" She, too, cared nothing for small waists.

Alimando enjoyed his mother's approval, but he found the infant overwhelming. What to do with such a small, helpless creature? He left baby care to Milma, while he spent long hours in the store and evenings out with his friends. When he received an invitation to the members-only Knights of Columbus, he couldn't conceal his pride. Acceptance by the local Italian community was worth more than a baby to Allie. He donned the K of C regalia and regarded himself in the mirror with satisfaction.

"Milma, I have a meeting tonight. Don't wait up for me."

In Milma's parents' Apostolic household, alcohol had been strictly forbidden. To fit in as a Rugani, she had seen that it would be useful to accept a glass of wine. Her first few swallows were forced. She tried to project nonchalance, but it was hard to disguise her nervous excitement. What if her parents were right, and the tart drink proved to be sinful? Milma sipped slowly. Other than a mild dislike of the taste, she noticed nothing at first. After a few minutes, a warm softness filtered through her body. Not so bad. But when Francesco refilled her glass, she decided not to press her luck and left it untouched.

The next day she felt fine, maybe better than fine, happy and quite liberated. Soon Milma was accepting the proffered glass, and a refill, with pleasure. The Apostolics were wrong about alcohol, a delightful discovery she knew better than to share with her parents.

At first Milma drank only with the Ruganis, but over time she began to pour herself a glass at home, here and there, to take the edge off the strangeness of her new life. When the door closed behind Alimando the night he headed pridefully off to the Knights of Columbus, she reached for the bottle. When Allie returned, Milma was snoring in their bed.

Baby Frank was only a few months old when the telephone rang. It was the local school, telling Milma that her replacement teacher had eloped in a shotgun wedding and was moving to Chicago. "It's too late to hire a new teacher, and we need a long-term substitute. Would you come back, Milma? We need you!"

Hanging up the phone to think it over, Milma felt a rush of energy. The baby was fine and all, but a part of her had died when she left the classroom to get married. Her days were long and notably unstimulating. The classroom was her milieu. Would Allie allow it? Would it be acceptable to have babysitters take care of Frank? What would the grandmothers say?

Milma may have been reserved and quiet, but when she wanted something, she made a beeline. "Allie," she said that evening, "I had a call from the school today. They want me to teach again."

"I thought married women couldn't teach." Alimando took a forkful of Milma's meat and potatoes and glanced up at his wife.

"They said they are making an exception because it's an emergency. Allie, I would like to do this. We can get babysitters for Frank, and the money would make things easier, wouldn't it?"

This last was a mistake. "We do NOT have problems with money." Alimando grew angry. The heady days of prohibition-related profits were gone, and the store was surviving but not exactly thriving, a truth he did not need to hear from his wife.

But he cooled off quickly. It would, in fact, be useful to have a second income in the house. "You would still cook great meals like this one?" he quizzed Milma.

"Of course I would, Allie. School is done by the middle of the afternoon."

"And you can find babysitters?"

"I'm sure I can." Milma actually had no idea who she would ask to help, but in that moment she didn't care. She was consumed by her desire for the teaching job.

"Okay, then, give it a try. We'll call it an experiment and see how it goes."

Just like that, Milma's life was reinvigorated. She cobbled together a babysitting plan, using the two grandmothers and the friendlier of her neighbors. She resisted the pressure of her mother's disapproval, and she accepted the risk that Teopista would feel even more entitled than before to be involved in their lives. She felt only the slightest twinge as she said good-bye to the baby on her first day, and then she plunged into the classroom, glowing.

In 1941, Francesco had a heart attack. "Too much stress!" said his doctor. "Stop working so hard."

Pista and Cecco discussed their options. The obvious solution was to ask Alimando to take a greater role in managing the store. "You must hand over more responsibility, *caro*. I know you don't want to, but do it for me. I don't want to lose you!"

Cecco opened the books to his son and laid out the challenges they faced.

"I can handle it, Pa," Allie said. "You take it easy." He was too proud to admit he was intimidated by the responsibility of running the store. Nor was he able to object when his father looked over his shoulder every day and second-guessed his decisions. He bottled up his resentment and soldiered on.

When Frank was three years old, Allie came home with a slate blackboard he had salvaged from an old school. He still felt awkward around his son, but periodically thought maybe he should be a more involved father.

"Son, it's time to learn how to write your name."

In careful script from his school days, Allie wrote, "Frank Charles Rugani" on the board. "Now you do it."

Frank looked at his father. "I don't know how."

"That's okay, just copy what I did."

Frank picked up the chalk. With a three-year-old's dexterity, he made a few wiggly lines on the slate.

"You can do better than that! Watch me." Alimando wrote a curved R for Rugani.

Frank responded with a squiggle.

"Jeez, kid! You can't even write your own name!" Allie suddenly feared there was something wrong with his son.

"Milma!" He shouted across the house. "This kid is too goddamn dumb to write his own name!"

Frank started to cry, and Milma came running. She gathered her son in her arms and she started to cry, too. "You can't expect a three-year-old to write his name! He hasn't learned to print, never mind cursive! What's wrong with you?"

Alimando swore and left the house with a bang. Milma sat with her son, stroking his hair until they both calmed down.

Alimando was twenty-seven years old, an insecure father, in charge of a marginal grocery store and humiliated to be dependent on his better-educated wife's salary. In a fit of frustration, he headed over to the Halfway Tavern in Atlantic Mine. The Halfway was a popular watering hole run by the Gagnon family. Marie Gagnon was a flirty waitress at her uncle's tavern, and Allie enjoyed bantering with her. He was also drawn to her because beneath her lively exterior, he knew she was sad. Her husband, not yet thirty, had died in the war a few months before. Pretty much every bachelor, along with half the married men in the area, was chomping at the bit to ask her out after a suitable mourning period had passed. Allie did not intend to ask her out—not today, anyway—but after the incident that left his wife and son both in tears, he wanted someone easy to talk to, someone who would restore his faith in himself. Marie did not disappoint.

"Hey, Allie! What can I get you? The usual?"

"Yes, please, Marie. You look very pretty today, did you know that?"

Marie blushed. "I know you say that to all the girls," she said. "But thanks."

Alimando polished off three drinks, chatted up Marie, and took the edge off his frustration. "I'd better go home," he told her. "Thanks for being here when I needed you."

"My pleasure, Allie. You take care, now." Marie stood on tiptoes and gave Allie a peck on the cheek. That spot vibrated for hours afterward, leaving Alimando feeling a lot better.

So much better, in fact, that he found himself thinking of Marie when he should have been thinking of Milma. The next day his distraction increased, and didn't let up. He knew it was wrong, but one morning a few days later, on the pretext of running an errand for the store, Allie drove over to Marie's house in Atlantic Mine.

She was surprised, but maybe not too surprised, to see him.

"Come in, Allie," she said. "Would you like a drink?" He was more awkward at her home than at the bar. They chatted about the weather, agreed that news from Europe was horrible, and Marie asked how things were going at the store.

She had framed photographs displayed on a sideboard. Allie got up to examine these, and Marie joined him. "These are my parents, before they came down here for my father to work as a logger," she said. "This is my sister, who never got used to the U.P. She went back to live with our aunt and uncle in Quebec. Sometimes I envy her." They were standing so close together that Allie could smell her hair. Describing the next picture, her arm brushed his. He turned to her.

"Beautiful Marie."

Had she stepped away, he would have done the same and willed himself to be a gentleman. She didn't. She turned her face up toward his, with obvious desire. He kissed her, and she led him to the bedroom.

With that act, Alimando became an unfaithful husband. When he went home later in the day, he wondered whether he would be able to hide his excitement and guilt. He was on cloud nine, yet deeply ashamed.

To his relief, Milma did not appear to suspect anything. She had been reserved ever since the incident with Frank and the blackboard, but they functioned as usual. And so, as time passed, Alimando developed a double life. With Milma, he made every effort to act normal, but whenever an opportunity presented itself, he slipped over to Marie's house. Sometimes he was sure Milma knew, while other times he felt convinced she did not. One day he found her in tears, and was afraid to ask what was wrong. He put his arms around her and she sobbed on his shoulder. "I had a hard day at school," she said. "Tommy Niemi is a scoundrel." Perhaps she told the truth, but her tears seemed more intense than a recalcitrant student would warrant. They ate in silence that night, and when Allie told her he was going out to a meeting, Milma looked down at her plate.

At the store Alimando was more buoyant, more fun with the employees, and more flirty with the housewives who came in to shop. But with his mother, he could not maintain eye contact. When Marie came into the store, if Teopista were there, too, Allie headed down to the storeroom to check on inventory. Fooling the employees or even his wife seemed possible to Allie; fooling Teopista was out of the question.

Marie became a pressure release for Alimando. Whenever he'd had a bad day, or thought he might have one; when he'd failed to find a way to connect to his young son; when the price of beef went up higher than his customers would be willing to pay; he took refuge in Marie. In the process, he grew less interested in Milma. Inevitably, he began to fantasize about being married to Marie instead of Milma. Marie understood him, and she didn't have the fancy college degree that left him feeling second-class.

Allie was not a total cad and he was not the type to abandon his family. For at least a year, they all lived in an uneasy equilibrium. Milma did suspect her husband was unfaithful, but she did not confront him; Allie did not leave his wife for Marie; and Marie did not demand more than Allie could give her.

One afternoon Allie slipped over to Marie's for a little pressure relief. She sat him down on the sofa. "Allie, I gotta tell you something. I'm pregnant."

Before he could speak, she continued. "I've thought it over and I'm going to stay with my cousin in Chicago. You and I can't go on like this, and I'll do better if I start a new life somewhere else. We need to call it quits. So this is goodbye, Allie." Marie got through her speech but her face was crumpling.

Alimando put his head in his hands. He should have been prepared for news like this, but he'd grown accustomed to denial. He closed his eyes and took a breath.

"I will come with you," he said. "I'm responsible for this child, and I will take care of you both. We'll start a new life together."

"Allie, no! You have a family here that needs you. And you have the store. You stay here. I'll be fine."

Allie shook his head. "I don't want to stay here without you." He took Marie's shoulders and looked into her teary face. "I love you, Marie. I want to come with you. I'll get a divorce and we'll get married."

Marie started to cry in earnest now. "No, Allie, please. Divorce is a sin. I wouldn't be able to live with myself, and you wouldn't either. We were meant to have fun and that's all. It couldn't last and we both knew it. Please go now. This is the right thing to do." She turned away from him. "Go."

Alimando knew she was right, but he was stricken. He looked at her shaking back for a long minute, and left the house.

"What's up with the boss?"

The grocery store guys elbowed each other and glanced in Allie's direction. Alimando had been in a foul mood for days, in contrast to his prior exuberance. He barked orders and cut short their smoke breaks. Going to work was a lot less fun than it was before. And then, just like that, Alimando was gone.

Allie was known for being at the store promptly at seven a.m., six days a week. He never called in sick, never slacked off. So on an otherwise unremarkable Wednesday in June of 1945, when he hadn't arrived at the store by ten, Francesco climbed the stairs to the apartment he and Teopista shared, and found her in the kitchen.

"Pista, Allie hasn't shown up at the store. Did he say anything to you about going somewhere?"

"No, he did not."

"Where do you think he is?"

Teopista put down her rolling pin. "I don't know, but something's not right. I'm gonna find out."

Pista wiped her hands on her apron and lumbered down the stairs. No one was home at Allie and Milma's place next door. Milma was teaching and Frank must have been out with his babysitter. Teopista stood on the street and folded her arms over her ample girth, thinking. It had been obvious to her that her son was having an affair, and based on their odd behavior when Marie Gagnon came into the store, she guessed that Marie was the mistress. She'd said so to Cecco, who, typically, claimed not to have noticed a thing. It was also clear that the affair had recently gone south. Nothing else could explain Alimando's foul moods of late.

Pista doubted Milma knew anything. She was a nice enough girl, but she paid more attention to her classroom than to her husband. Even so, Pista thought she'd better start there. She smoothed her hair and walked a block to the school. Teopista's English was poor and the school intimidated her, but this couldn't wait. She opened the door and entered, for the first time in her life. No one was there to stop her, so she walked down the hall, looking inside each classroom until she found Milma.

"Pssst! Milma!"

Milma did a double take. What was her mother-in-law doing *here*, in her apron in the doorway to a classroom? The scene was incongruous. Something must be very wrong. She excused herself to her class and went to the door. "What is it, Ma?"

"Milma, do you know where Alimando is?"

"Isn't he at the store?"

"No, he never showed up this morning."

"Well, I don't know. He was at home this morning, as usual. Maybe he went out to talk to a supplier?"

Teopista shook her head. "Not possible. Okay, we continue to look."

The students rustled. "I can't leave now, but I'll come by later," Milma said. "I hope it's nothing." Privately, she wondered whether her husband was with his mistress. It was obvious to her that he had one, though she wasn't sure who it was. In that moment, she kept her suspicion to herself. She wasn't going to risk being overheard discussing something so personal, never mind starting to cry, at school. She pulled herself together and restored order to her classroom.

Teopista was determined to find her son. She began with her theory that Marie had jilted him and he was drowning his sorrows somewhere. Geno Lucchesi might know. He was the closest thing Allie had to a real friend. Pista marched over to the Range Oil and Gas Company and found Geno.

"Geno, have you seen Alimando? He didn't show up for work this morning."

"*Buon giorno, signora,*" Geno greeted her. "Allie? Gee, no, I dunno where he is."

"Geno, I know Alimando was having an affair, so don't pretend he wasn't. I suspect Marie Gagnon, am I right?"

Geno shrugged. "Aww, I don't know. No, I don't think so."

"Come on, Geno. Something happened between them. Did she cut him off? You look me straight in the eye and you tell me." Pista never trusted a man who couldn't look her straight in the eye.

Geno couldn't hold her gaze. "Mrs. Rugani, I really don't know. They had some kind of argument, I think that's all."

Teopista glared at Geno. "I'm thinking you know more than you're saying. Geno Lucchesi." Pista was a force when she wanted something.

"I don't know, I swear!" Geno prayed that this conversation would come to a close.

Teopista shook her head. "I'll be back to talk to you again, Geno, unless you see the light and decide you're gonna come tell me everything you know." She turned around to leave and Geno wiped his brow.

When the school day ended, Milma stopped by the store. "Has Allie shown up?"

"No, he hasn't," said Francesco. "Pista is on the warpath, looking for him. I figure he's probably just taking a little time to himself. Let's not worry yet, okay, Milma?"

"Yeah, okay. It's probably nothing. Thanks, Pa. Milma went next door to her son and sent the babysitter home. She spent the afternoon playing with Frank and preparing dinner, wondering whether her husband would return to eat it. He didn't.

The next day was Saturday, no school. Milma had just finished her coffee when Teopista knocked on her door. "No Alimando last night, eh? Okay. I talked to everyone in South Range yesterday, and no one claimed to know anything. We gotta find him, Milma. He can't just run away from his family and the store, no? Come with me to Atlantic Mine. We go talk to that no-good Frenchman Gagnon."

Milma regarded her charged-up mother-in-law. The last thing she felt like doing was facing the family of her husband's mistress, if that's who the Gagnons were. The humiliation was too great. "You know, Ma, I'd like to give him a couple of days. He's probably just clearing his head somewhere. He'll be back."

"*Cara*, think about this! Your husband had an affair – you know it and I know it – and now he's gone. This is not right. Don't be the passive wife and let him get away with this. He probably had the affair in the first place because you don't stand up for yourself."

Milma's eyes filled. "Ma! What are you saying?" Her lip trembled. "I'm sorry, but you need to leave my house now. My marriage is my business, not yours." Milma stood up from the table. "Please go."

Teopista saw she had overstepped. "Look, I'm sorry, Milma. I shouldn't have said that. I'm worried about him, that's all."

"Please go," said Milma, trying not to cry.

Teopista patted her on the shoulder and Milma closed her eyes. "Okay, we talk later," said Pista. "I am sorry, *cara*."

When her mother-in-law was gone, Milma stopped holding back the tears. How had her life come to this? Her parents had been right—marrying the Italian grocer was a mistake. He was unfaithful and now he was gone. Part of her wanted him back, while another part hoped he would never return. Good riddance. She could move somewhere else and start over. But. She did still want him, sort of, and where would she go? Her whole life had been spent within a few miles of South Range, Michigan. Milma sobbed harder.

And then, five-year-old Frank nervously approached. "Mama? What's the matter?"

"Oh, honey." Milma wiped her eyes. "I'm sorry. Don't worry, everything is okay." She didn't know how much her son understood of the situation, but she needed to communicate strength to him.

"I want to go see Nonno at the store," said Frank. "Can I go?"

Milma felt the tears well up again. Her own son didn't even want to be with her. She took a deep breath. "Yes, you can go." Frank loved spending time with his grandfather at the store. He needed comfort today, and Nonno would provide it. But why wasn't it good enough for Frank to be with her, his mother? She let out another sob. "Go ahead, now, that's a good boy." Frank looked at her uncertainly, and then ran out the door.

That afternoon, Teopista squeezed behind the wheel of the car. She didn't drive often, but today she was on a mission. With both hands on the wheel, she steered over to Atlantic Mine and pulled into the parking lot of the Halfway Tavern. The place was full of Saturday drinkers. The music was loud and the crowd louder. Heavily made-up waitresses circulated with trays of drinks, leaning into their grinning customers as they took orders and accepted tips with a wink.

Teopista had never been to such a place. She'd had raucous parties in her own living room, and the bar reminded her a little bit of her youth in Monsegrati, but now, with her shabby floral dress and swollen ankles, she was not in her element. A few heads turned when she entered, but no one spoke to her.

She approached the bar and asked for "Signore Gagnon, please."

"Hey, boss, there's an Italian lady here to see you!"

A mustached, middle-aged man came out from the back, wiping his hands on his apron. He cocked his head when he saw Teopista. "May I help you?"

"*Signore*, I am Mrs. Rugani, mother of Alimando. Your niece is Marie Gagnon, yes?"

"Yes, that's right. Wait, you said Rugani?"

Teopista nodded.

"Rugani! You are the mother of the reason our Marie has left us!" Gagnon narrowed his eyes. "Why are you here?"

"Believe me, sir, I could not be more sorry about what has happened. I am here to see if we might work together." Teopista had not forgotten how to charm a man in a difficult situation, and he'd already given her the valuable information that Marie had also left. "Mr. Gagnon, this is a nice bar. You are running a good business here, I can tell."

Gagnon softened a little bit. "Thank you. We work hard here."

"Ruganis know about hard work, too. We have devoted ourselves to our business, as you have. And to our family – nothing is more important than family, don't you think?"

"Yes, ma'am. The Gagnons are a close family."

"Ruganis too," said Teopista, exaggerating only a little. "And every family has its troubles, I know. Some years ago I lost my first-born son, Giuseppe. He was a virtuoso violin player, just fifteen years old, when he got sick and died." Pista grew teary with the memory.

"I am sorry, Mrs. Rugani. That's terrible."

Teopista nodded. "Thank you." She looked up at Mr. Gagnon. "May I ask you a big favor?" He nodded.

"Can you tell me where your Marie is? Alimando is now missing, and I have a bad feeling he went to her. Something happened between them, but I don't know the story." Pista got out a handkerchief and dabbed her eyes. "I am so worried, now, about both of them. If you are worried, too, maybe you can help me."

Mr. Gagnon was tempted to toss Teopista out on her ear. Why should he help the mother of that philandering grocer who knocked up their Marie? But it was not so easy to dismiss Teopista Rugani. She was a force, and he felt sympathy for her, despite himself. He was also just a little worried about what she might do if he declined to help her.

The morning he didn't show up at the store, Alimando had gone over to Marie's mother's house in Atlantic Mine. "Mrs. Gagnon, I'm sorry to bother you, but do you have Marie's address in Chicago? I want to send her a card."

Mrs. Gagnon sighed. "Alimando, Marie left to get away from

you. If you had stayed out of her life, she would still be here where she belongs."

Alimando touched his hand to his heart. "I apologize, Mrs. Gagnon. Believe me, I miss her, too. All I want to do is send her a card telling her I'm sorry. Could you please just tell me where I can send it? It would mean the world to me." Allie looked stricken, and Mrs. Gagnon relented. She wrote down an address in Chicago and handed Allie the paper.

"Thank you, ma'am," said Allie. He headed home but didn't go inside, where Frank was playing with his babysitter. He went around the side of the house where he had stashed a suitcase, and then walked quickly to the train station. He had a story ready in case he saw anyone he knew, but he got lucky. The train for Chicago left promptly at 8:30 a.m., with Allie Rugani aboard. He had to see Marie.

Once in Chicago, Alimando went to a pay phone and dialed the number of his friend Guido, who had moved to the city a few years ago. "Guido, it's Allie Rugani. I'm in Chicago, and I wonder if you could do me a huge favor."

Guido came through for his old friend. He was homesick for the Copper Country, and he didn't mind taking in a guest. He and Allie embraced.

Climbing the stairs to a fourth-floor walkup apartment in the Little Italy neighborhood, Guido warned his friend: "The place ain't much, but it's home. You can sleep on the sofa."

"Thanks, Guido. I owe you." Over a drink they shared stories. Like many Italians from Lucca, Guido worked as a plasterer. The work was messy, but safer than many construction jobs. "When I stay out of the bar, if you know what I mean, I can save up some real money. One day I'll meet the right girl and start a family. Like you, Allie."

Allie regarded his friend. "Here's the thing, Guido. God knows I love my wife and my son, more than life itself. But there's also this girl, Marie. You should see how beautiful she is, God help me. I came here because I have to see her. *Capisce?* Do you understand what I'm saying?"

Guido nodded. "Sure, Allie. I know what you're saying. You

were always the big man around town. Some of us got no girl at all, and you got two. Lucky bastard."

"Not so lucky now, though. Marie got pregnant and came down here to have the baby. I couldn't talk her out of leaving town. And now I'm going crazy without her." Alimando pulled out the carefully folded paper with Marie's address and showed it to Guido. "Do you know where this is?"

"Yeah, I know the street. Couple miles from here. Turn left out the door, first right, then several blocks down. You'll find it."

"Okay, thanks!" Allie jumped up from the table and clapped his friend on the back. He ran his fingers through his hair and adjusted his belt. "I'll be back – wish me luck!"

Alimando stopped at a flower cart to buy the biggest bouquet they had, and then followed Guido's directions to Marie's cousin's apartment. When he saw three unfamiliar surnames on the doorbells at the street level, he realized he didn't know which one was her cousin. Rather than waste time trying them one by one, he rang all three. The ground-level door opened, and heads popped out of windows on the second and third floors.

"I'm looking for Marie Gagnon!" Allie looked up and spoke to all of them at once. Two people shrugged, while the woman on the top floor quickly pulled her head back inside. A moment later she reappeared. "She's not here," the woman called down, "and she doesn't want to see you."

Alimando wasn't going to give up easily. "I know she's in there! Tell her please, just let me say hello. I'll be gone in five minutes."

The head disappeared and then reappeared. "I told you she's not here."

"Marie!!" Alimando shouted up to the open window. "I got something for you. If I can't come up there, why don't you come down to the door? I won't even come in. Please?!"

The woman in the window shook her head. "Please leave."

"Okay," said Alimando. "These flowers are for Marie. I'm leaving them at the door here and I'll walk away. If you don't come down and get them, someone else is sure gonna have a nice bouquet."

For the next two days, this scene repeated itself. Allie was rebuffed via a head out the window, and he left his floral offering at the door, adding notes to Marie in an effort to get a foot in the door.

On the fourth day, she relented. Instead the stranger's head appearing out the window, it was Marie's. Alimando was overjoyed.

"Marie! Can I come up for a minute? Or will you come down?"

"I'll come down, Allie, but you can't stay."

Marie and Allie ended up sitting on the stoop, talking. Allie told her he was sleeping on his friend Guido's couch, and Marie said her cousin had given her the only bed, due to her condition.

"How are ya feeling, Marie?" he asked her. "You look beautiful."

"I don't feel too good, if you want to know. People say it gets better after a while. I sure hope so." Marie looked down.

"You'd make me the happiest man on earth if you'd let me take care of you and the baby," said Allie. "I'm responsible for this little one, and I'm in love with you."

Marie sighed. "That's nice of you to say, Allie. But it wouldn't work between us. You have a family already, and you have the store. There's no place for me in any of that."

"We don't have to go back to South Range, Marie! There are guys at the store who can help my father run it—do all the heavy stuff that he can't do. They'll be fine. And Milma, she'd be fine, too. She has her own job and she has family at the farm to help with the boy. She and I aren't right for each other, Marie, not like you and me. We could go anywhere, and start over! What do you say?"

"What would you even do for work, Allie? All you've known is the store."

"Well, I'm sure I could find a grocery store that needed some help. Maybe even one that we could buy for ourselves one day." Allie allowed himself to get hopeful, and he turned on the charm for Marie. "A place of our own! No more ball and chain of the family business, no more being bossed around by my father and examined every minute by Teopista. Let's do it, Marie!"

"Aww, Allie, I don't think it would work. But I do appreciate that you care."

"Just promise me you'll think it over, Marie. I'll come back tomorrow and we can talk again. Maybe go for a walk, okay?"

"Thanks for the flowers," said Marie. "I'm going back in now."

In the following days Alimando continued, unsuccessfully, to convince Marie to run away with him. He made it his mission in life to prevail. Each night he returned to Guido's place to plot his next move. One evening, Guido's phone rang.

Allie got excited. "It must be Marie, calling to say yes! Answer it, Guido!" It was not Marie. Alimando heard his friend fumble a few words in Italian, and then Guido put his hand over the receiver. With wide eyes he whispered, "It's your mother!"

Allie panicked. "How did she find me? Tell her I'm not here," he whispered back.

"He's not here, Mrs. Rugani. I'm not sure where he went. What? Yes, okay, I'll tell him you called."

Alimando immediately regretted his error. Why didn't he tell Guido to say he hadn't seen him? He lowered his forehead into his palm. He was never good at lying to his mother, or even getting someone else to lie for him.

"I need a drink," he said to Guido, who was already pouring two glasses. Teopista had Guido twisted in a knot, too.

"Oh, my God." Allie shook his head. "How about we stop answering the phone for the next month?" His laugh was hollow.

The next time Teopista called, she told Guido she would get on a train and come to Chicago personally if he didn't put

Alimando on the phone. Guido gave in.

"Alimando," said Teopista, "what in God's name do you think you are doing? I have prayed to the Virgin Mary for a week that you would come home to your family and the store where you belong, but my prayers have gone unanswered. You are doing wrong, Alimando, and you know it. I did not raise my son to abandon his family. If you don't put yourself on the next train home, I will do as I said to Guido—I will come down there myself and drag you down the street by your hair. No joke. Get yourself back here, Alimando. Be a man."

That night, Allie stared at the ceiling. His life was a mess. Marie wouldn't take him, and his mother had laid bare his failings. He remembered his invincible younger days, and hardly recognized that tough, confident version of himself. All night long, his mother's reproaches echoed in his head, until he knew what he had to do.

"Guido," Allie said in the morning, "I have no choice. I'm going back."

Alimando's first stop in South Range was the store, where Teopista embraced him.

"Good boy. I know this was not easy for you. Now we will say no more about it." Having gotten what she wanted, Pista let her son off the hook. She needed him in his rightful place in the family, and she needed him to regain his confidence. There would be no more recrimination over his bad behavior.

Reconciliation with Milma was not so easy. She suffered from layers of hurt and anger that were not going to dissolve overnight. After a few drinks—an increasingly frequent occurrence in the evening—she would grow either angry or soft, unpredictably. Alimando knew he held no cards in this game, which made him maddeningly powerless. And he was heartbroken over his loss of Marie, a state he couldn't confess to anyone except Geno.

One afternoon, Allie stepped outside the store for some air. A curl of smoke was rising from behind the garage of their home next door. He ran over, and saw a fire starting to spread.

"Fire!" he yelled. "Call the fire department!"

Running away from the blaze were two young boys. One was five-year-old Frank, who knew how to use matches because he'd been taught to light the water heater in the basement. In an instant, after days of restraint and depression, Allie blew up. He ran to his son, grabbed him by the arm, and lifted him off the ground. Whaling on Frank's behind the whole way, he hauled the screaming boy from the garage to the house and straight up to his second-floor bedroom. "Welcome to High Mass with no organ, you stupid kid!" This had been a favorite phrase of Alimando's since he'd first heard it down at the bar. Music was the only thing that made Mass tolerable; little boys who started fires got all the pain of the sermon and none of the pleasure of the music.

The whole neighborhood came out for the spectacle: Allie whacking his son within an inch of his life; Frank screaming with pain, guilt, and fear; smoke rising from behind the garage; and finally sirens drowning out Frank's screams as the local department arrived and doused the fire.

Allie threw his son onto the bed. "You will not move from here until tomorrow," Allie instructed his son. "Use the time to think over how stupid you just were."

On his way out the bedroom door, Alimando turned back to Frank. "And another thing. As of today you are no longer the mascot for the fire department. That job was an honor, and you do not deserve any honor." One of the excitements of Frank's life had been to put on his miniature firefighter's outfit, complete with helmet, and ride on the department's trucks in local parades. Frank cried even harder.

With a small boy's sobs in the background, Allie found Milma in the kitchen, staring out the window. "And what about you? Were you paying no attention to your own son? He could have burned the whole place down!"

It was Milma's turn to snap. "Of course I feel badly about the fire, Alimando! What do you think? I figured our son was smart enough not to do that, and I was wrong. So I'm sorry!"

She turned toward him. "But," she said, "don't you think you are over-reacting? You want to starve our son and punish him this harshly for making a childish mistake? If he hates you some day, you know, it will be your own fault."

"Milma! How dare you?" Alimando turned a brighter shade of red than he was already.

Milma was taken aback by her own words, too, and she backed off a little. "I'm sorry, Allie, but Frank is just a boy. Didn't you ever do something stupid when you were that young? You must have."

"I certainly did not just about burn my whole house down!" he said. "Our son has to learn responsibility. How else will he get along in the world?"

"Allie, he's five years old. He will learn as he grows."

The result of this sorry episode was that Frank spent even more time next door at the store with Pista and Cecco, his Ma and Nonno. Nonno took him down to the basement to pack eggs into cartons and peel the loose skins off onions so they would look better on display. Frank loved having these jobs to do, even when he and Nonno maintained a companionable silence as they worked.

With Ma there was never silence, nor was life predictable. One warm evening, Frank and Teopista were sitting on a bench in front of the store. Across the street at the community hall, a band was playing dance music. Teopista began tapping her feet and swaying her body. Suddenly she jumped up.

"Franchino! Let's go to the dance!"

She took off her apron and grabbed Frank by the hand.

"I don't know how to dance, Ma!"

"No problem, Franchino, I show you."

Pista was so excited she practically skipped across the street, which given her bulk, was a sight. Inside the hall, she pulled Frank onto the dance floor. She took his right hand and clamped it under her pillowy arm.

"Now hold your other hand out here." She took his small left hand in her big right one.

"Good! Now, follow me." Teopista waltzed her grandson around the floor. He stumbled so much that they both burst out laughing. "Isn't this wonderful, Franchino?" She gave a full-throated laugh. "There is nothing better than to dance!"

Frank thought there was nothing better than to be enveloped in the buxom love of his grandmother. He basked in her warmth and joy, and neither of them cared that he had no idea what he was doing.

Allie, Milma, and Frank eventually settled into a new normal. After two of his letters to Marie were returned unopened, Allie accepted that she would not be allowing him into her life, and probably not the life of the baby when it arrived, either. As he let Marie go, he devoted more attention to his family, and they responded. Milma started to believe that her husband was back, and she warmed up. Once she stopped being acutely hurt and angry, she allowed the possibility of intimacy again, and after a long hiatus, she became pregnant for the second time.

Frank felt the difference in the household and he grew happier, too. His father could be expansive and affectionate, and when Frank did something well, Allie praised him to anyone who'd listen. Alimando enjoyed the role of proud papa to his first-born son.

One night, when Frank was seven years old, Allie came home with a bicycle.

"Son, you're doing so well in school that I brought you a present. It's time you had a bicycle. We'll go outside after dinner and I'll show you how to ride it."

Frank's response was muted, and Allie narrowed his eyes a little. "Aren't you excited, son?"

"Yeah, Dad, sure I am. Thank you."

After dinner they went out to the sidewalk and Allie sat his son on the bicycle seat. His feet barely reached the pedals. "Okay, I'm going to push you along until you get going," said Allie, "and then you start pedaling." He ran alongside the bike with his hand on the seat, and once Frank had some momentum, he gave him a shove and let go.

Frank careened down the sidewalk for a few seconds, and then lost his balance and fell over.

"Frankie, you gotta keep pedaling. Otherwise you'll fall over, okay? Let's try again."

Back in the other direction, Allie ran alongside the bicycle before giving Frank a push and letting go. Frank didn't last much longer on this second attempt, before falling again and skinning his knee. Allie didn't notice, or didn't want to notice, that his son was fighting back tears.

"Come on, Frank, you can do better than that! Get back on the bike."

Frank was tense and in pain at this point, with the inevitable result that he fell even sooner on the third attempt. With blood running down both legs, he started to cry. Alimando lost his temper. "What kid can't even ride a bike? How can you be so uncoordinated? Geez!"

"I don't want a bike! I never wanted a bike!" yelled Frank. "Leave me alone!"

"You stupid kid!" Allie yelled right back. "I thought you should have a bike, but you're too goddamn dumb to ride it! Stop sniveling and go put it away."

Allie strode back into the house while Frank, blinded by tears and shamed in front of the whole street, rolled the bike into the garage. Inside the house, Milma had a warm cloth ready to clean him up. "Allie, really! What were you thinking?" She tried simultaneously to comfort her son and scold her husband, but Alimando was already heading out the door with the car keys, not bothering to tell them where he was going.

The incident was a setback for the family's fragile peace process. Milma had given birth to a daughter, and was pregnant with a third child, but she was drinking more. Alimando was as volatile as ever—warm and affectionate one day, angry and out at the bar the next. Grocery store business was steady, but the hours were long and no one was going to get rich selling groceries in South Range.

On Saturday nights, Pista and Cecco invited family and friends to their apartment above the store. Teopista used these occasions to rally her family.

"Let's roll back the carpet," she said. "If you have an instrument, play it! If you no play, you dance!"

Alimando brought his accordion, and neighbors came with fiddles and a clarinet. Frank served drinks, which his father had taught him to do by age five. It felt good to be thanked for bringing someone a full glass. Frank started thinking he might want to be a bartender.

"A bartender!" Teopista fed *biscotti* and milk to Frank one day after school. "Franchino, listen to me. There is a wide world out there. You are destined to be something much more than a bartender. You keep doing good in school, you go to college, and you do something great. No more talk of bartender, okay?"

"Okay, Ma," said Frank, with no idea what could be more great than being thanked for bringing someone a drink. He'd ruled out being a fireman after the incident behind the garage. His mother was a teacher and he liked his teachers at school— maybe he could do that. But they were all women. Frank quietly began to worry about what he should do when he grew up.

⚜

Teopista loved the movies, even though she didn't understand most of the English words. "Franchino," she said, "tonight we go to the movies, you and me."

After the credits rolled, she asked Frank what the movie was about. He told her, and she responded with her version. "It was a love story," she said, even though it wasn't. She had a dreamy look on her face, and even at age seven, Frank knew better than to contradict her.

The next Friday, Pista wanted to go to the theater again. Midway through the movie, Frank tugged on her arm. "Ma, I have to go to the bathroom."

Pista was totally engrossed in the story. "Shhh. Wait 'til the movie's over."

"I can't wait, Ma. I really gotta go," he whispered.

She didn't take her eyes from the screen. "Just pee here," she said.

"Here?" Frank was chagrined.

"Yes, now be quiet!"

Mortified, Frank peed in his seat. The next time they went to the movies, Pista got a Mason jar out of the cupboard.

"Tonight, Franchino, if you gotta pee, use this." He did, and Teopista watched her love story uninterrupted.

Frank was seven and eight years old when Milma gave birth to two baby girls, one year after the other. She took only a minimal maternity leave and then went right back to the classroom. Teaching was the only thing between Milma and alcoholism, and some part of her knew it. Staying at home with young children all day was not for her.

However, it was harder to find good babysitters for two young children than it had been when it was just Frank. Teopista and Teresia helped, but there was a gap.

"We will hire Cora Battistoni," said Alimando.

"We most certainly will not!" said Milma. Cora's nickname in town was *Zia Fiana,* Aunt Witch. Stories about Fiana had traveled up one side of the town and down the other.

"Fiana has had three husbands, and she killed two of them!" a neighbor said to Milma.

"No."

"Yes. The first one was a miner who walked up the hill to Quincy Mine every night. One very stormy night, he told Cora it was too snowy to go out, but she packed his lunch and said he had to go or else they'd have nothing to eat. They didn't find him until spring, frozen to death in a snow bank."

Milma's eyes widened.

"The next one was even worse. He was sitting at the breakfast table when he pulled out a pistol and pointed it to his own head. 'Somebody told me,' he said to Fiana, 'that you don't love me anymore. You'd better tell me you love me, or I'm going to kill myself.'

"So what does she say? She says, 'They were right, I hate you, you sonofabitch.' So he blew his brains out and fell into his scrambled eggs."

Milma hung on every word as the neighbor went on. "That's not all. Fiana burns down her houses for the insurance money. She even set her own candy store on fire. The building wasn't damaged very much when the fire department arrived, so she pulled a few gallons of wine out of the basement, and pretty soon the firemen were having a party instead of putting out the fire. Fiana got her insurance money."

Milma went straight home. "Allie, this woman cannot go anywhere near our children."

"Milma, those are just stories. Cora did Ma and Pa a big favor when they wanted to get married, and we owe her. Plus, don't forget Ruby. A bad person would not have done what Cora did for Ruby."

Cora had been at the counter of her candy store one day when a woman came in with a baby buggy. She told Cora she had to run to the post office for a quick minute, and asked if Cora would watch the baby. Cora agreed, and when she took a look into the carriage, she saw a little black girl. No one for miles around had ever seen a black baby.

"The baby was wet," Allie told Milma, "and Cora rigged up a diaper with a dishtowel. Then the lady never came back! So what did Cora do? She decided to raise that baby on her own. She named her Ruby, and she gave her a good life. Only a heart of gold would do that, right?"

Alimando insisted, and since Milma had no other options, she agreed. But she hated to hear her children call Cora "Zia."

"She is not your aunt!"

In the end, nobody was murdered and Cora did fine with the girls. Milma decided not to argue when Cora took home leftover food in an empty babyfood jar, which she ate on dishes she'd stolen one by one from a diner. Cora needed the food and the job, and Milma needed the babysitting.

Frank always remembered Cora because each time he went to her apartment to ask her to come babysit, she handed him a shoe.

"Frankie, help me. I got cock-a-roaches in here. You kill the cock-a-roaches, like a good boy, okay?"

After Frank whacked a couple of cockroaches with the shoe, Cora would agree to come over to babysit.

There was one holy hour each week in Alimando's home. It was Sunday nights, when the *Horace Height Amateur Hour* came on the radio. If the accordion player Dick Contino was on the show, Allie required absolute silence in the household for as long as Contino played. If a baby cried, Allie glared and Milma rushed the baby out of the room.

Dick Contino was playing the night that Allie's sister Rose Notari came bursting into the house in tears. "Allie, you have to help me! My husband is dying in the sanitarium, and he got a priest to rewrite his will so all his money will go to Italy, with none for me!" Rose wailed.

Alimando held up his hand and said, perfectly calmly, "Rose, you will wait until my program is over." He leaned back in his chair and closed his eyes with a blissful look on his face, ignoring Rose, who tried to stifle her gasping sobs. The music went on and on, and when it was finally over, Allie turned off the radio and said, "Okay, tell me that again."

Rose blubbered out her tale a second time, and Allie said, "This is not acceptable. Rose, get in the car. We're going down to Marquette." At nine o'clock in the evening, Allie drove Rose nearly two hours to the sanitarium where her husband lay struggling to breathe. Their first stop was the rectory, where

Allie roused the priest out of his bed. "Father, we are taking you to the sanitarium right now to rewrite Mr. Notari's will. My sister will not be left out."

The priest squinted at Allie and ran his fingers through what was left of his hair. "Take it easy there, pal. We can go in the morning."

Allie grabbed him by the arm. "No, we are going now. The only question you need to answer is whether you want to put your trousers on, or whether you want to go in your pajamas." He allowed the priest to get dressed, and then dragged him by the arm to the car and threw him in the back seat. Alimando was so worked up that he damaged the car door getting it open, and he drove like a madman to the sanitarium.

When they arrived, they found Rose's husband, Anthony Notari, in an oxygen tent. Notari was one of the founders of the Stella Cheese Company in Baltic, and he had done quite well for himself. "Notari," said Alimando, "the Father here and I have come because we're changing your will back. We know that you want to leave everything to your wife, my sister Rose. Is that not right?"

Notari shook his head, "No."

"No?"

Alimando stepped on Notari's oxygen hose. When he began gasping for air, Allie took his foot off and said, "Notari, maybe you didn't understand me. We're here to rewrite the will." Again Notari shook his head, and again Allie stepped on the hose. Notari began to gasp more frantically, and finally he waved his hand in surrender. He signed the papers, whereupon the priest said, "Okay, I guess that's all then, right?"

"No," said Allie, "there's one more thing. I am taking you home. You came with me and you will leave with me."

"Please, no," said the priest. "No more riding in that car!" But Alimando forcibly led him outside and gave him another angry ride next to a door that didn't close completely. Notari died the next morning. Mission accomplished.

When Allie thought something should happen, he didn't take no for an answer. He hated injustice and was willing to use force or intimidation to correct it. He had done the same thing when thugs tried to overturn his truck or steal his money. He was raised in a Mafia-like environment and he behaved accordingly. He bullied for justice.

All his life, Alimando hated to lose, and he resented any intimation that he and his family were second-class. His father, Cecco, seemed to accept his place in the hierarchy of Italian society. The grocery store was a big step up from laboring underground in the mines, and Cecco had no ambition to rise further. Alimando, by contrast, was a restless soul.

Now and then he wondered how his life would have been different had he gone to college. But the point was moot. Alimando was powerless to raise his family's status in any meaningful way. He had married an educated girl, but she would forever be a *filandra,* an outsider incapable of changing the Italian community's view of the Ruganis. The one thing Allie could do, he came to realize, was to make good and sure that his son succeeded. Alimando focused his ambitions on Frank.

One night he came home with a 48-bass accordion in a box. He showed it to Frank, and said, "It's time you became an accordion player. I've set up your first lesson for tomorrow night, with David Pizzi."

"Gee, Dad, I don't know if I want to play the accordion," Frank said. At age ten, Frank still hadn't accepted that his father rarely offered him a choice.

"You're going to play," Allie said, "and you're going to take lessons from David Pizzi."

Frank plugged away at the instrument, wondering how the Italians could love it so much. The right hand plays a keyboard, the left hand works the buttons, and the player pumps bellows at the same time. For all that effort, the sound that comes out is like a sick donkey, even when its done right, which takes a long time to master.

David Pizzi wasn't a very good teacher, and Frank's progress was slow. Allie insisted he continue, even as he criticized Frank's rhythm. He decided the problem was David Pizzi, so he found a new teacher in the town of Hubbell, instructing Milma to drive Frank ten miles there and back each week. Then he decided Frank needed a better instrument, so he raided his son's bank account—where Frank had painstakingly squirreled away $500 by saving every gift he ever received—and spent the money on a 120-bass accordion.

Milma was shocked. "Allie! That money was not yours to spend!"

"The kid doesn't know what's good for him," said Alimando. "He'll thank me later, when he understands the value of a decent instrument. I found him a new teacher, too. He will start with Peter Ciucci in Hancock on Monday."

Frank fought back tears. "You took my money!" The tears spilled out despite his efforts to suppress them. He wailed and ran upstairs to his room.

Alimando yelled after him, "I spent all day getting you this fine instrument! Now stop sniveling!"

"Alimando, you stop!" Milma hissed. "You have learned nothing about children. Why do you keep hurting our son?"

"You don't understand, either, do you? The boy needs to toughen up and learn to play. A little pain now will bring him a lifetime of benefit. Why is everyone against me in this household?"

Milma poured herself a drink. "Just stop and think for a moment. If your father had taken your money to buy you an instrument you didn't want, how would you have reacted? I'll bet you would have thrown that expensive accordion right through the window."

Allie lost his temper. "Frank is only upset because *you* have put soft ideas in his head! Now shut your mouth and support your husband!" The door banged behind him as he left for the evening.

That Monday, and every Monday for the rest of the school year, Frank hoisted his new accordion into the back seat of the car and Milma drove him twenty minutes to Peter Ciucci's home in Hancock. Neither of them dared defy Alimando. The saving grace of the arrangement was that Peter was a kind and patient teacher. Frank learned to play the accordion, despite his resentment of his father for stealing his money and forcing him to play.

When people came over to the house, Alimando was a proud papa. "Frank, go get your accordion and show our guests how you can play 'The Sharpshooter's March.'" Quietly, to Frank, he said, "Hit all the notes and make sure you get the bellows right." Frank did what he could, and even when he was imperfect, Allie beamed. "Good job, son!" Everyone exhaled.

When she married Alimando, Milma had converted to Catholicism and proceeded to practice her faith with the zeal of a convert. She knew every word of the catechism, and the family never missed church. Alimando felt a little pressured by her enthusiasm, but his mother was delighted.

"Allie," said Pista, "see what a good woman you married? She never miss church. Good girl!"

"Yeah, Ma, I know." Allie busied himself behind the butcher's counter while Pista smiled with satisfaction. Then she had an idea.

"I'm gonna go say hello to Milma," she said to Allie, "and tell her how happy I am that she love the church."

Next door she gave her daughter-in-law a pillowy embrace. "Milma, I been thinking. It's time for Frank to become an altar boy! Isn't that a good idea? Let's go see Father Shulek right now and ask him."

Milma needed no convincing. She could please her mother-in-law and be proud of her son, all at once. It was a rare moment of congruence in her challenging life.

At the church, Teopista looked Father Shulek straight in the eye. "Father, we want you to take on our Franchino as an altar boy. He's a good boy and he loves the church. Okay?"

Fortunately for Father Shulek, he had no objection. Saying no to Teopista Rugani would not have been a happy experience. "Sure, Teopista, he can start on Sunday."

"Frank," Milma said the moment she got home, "Father Shulek is extending you the great honor of serving as an altar boy. Isn't that wonderful?"

Frank swallowed. "Okay, Mom. But what does an altar

boy do?"

Fortunately for Frank, Father Shulek was a good man. He praised Frank for doing a good job with the vestments, and Frank beamed. Milma and Pista and Cecco also beamed, and Frank began to think he might want to become a priest.

As the wife of a member of the Sons of Italy, regardless of her heritage, Milma was eligible to join the Daughters of Italy. She was nearly the only Finnish member, but she didn't care. She threw herself into club activities and helped out with every event. Fundraisers and sewing circles and theater productions staved off her loneliness, and, just maybe, she thought, Alimando would be proud of her and less inclined to indulge his wandering eye. Her efforts didn't change her marriage, but she did enjoy the company. The Daughters could be bawdy and loud, and with a glass of wine or two for lubrication, so could Milma.

When Frank was eleven years old, Milma asked him to play his accordion during the intermission of a Daughters of Italy Christmas play. By then he was used to being pressed into service, and he didn't protest. He struck up a waltz, and wasn't four measures into the piece when his grandmother jumped up from the audience. By herself, Pista began to dance around the hall with a rapturous look on her face. When the piece was over, she planted a big wet kiss on Frank's cheek. "Franchino, that was so wonderful. I'm gonna give-a you some money, so you go buy something for yourself tomorrow." Frank got that warm feeling inside that only Pista could generate. Later, he suspected that she had known about the raided bank account and the coerced music lessons, and was compensating for the sins of her son. She didn't miss much that went on in her family. In the moment, though, all he knew was that he had made his grandmother deeply happy, and for once in the whole sad saga of the accordion, he was glad he knew how to play it.

Loppeglia and Torcigliano Alto, Tuscany

One day in May of 1952, a letter arrived from Italy for Teopista and Cecco. Pista read it from beginning to end, read it again, and looked up with fire in her eyes. It was from Cecco's sister-in-law Oenesta, who wrote that she had had a dream that Cecco and Pista came to Italy to visit, bringing their grandson Franchino with them. "And so, you must come," Oenesta wrote. "You must fulfill my dream."

"Cecco, we will go to Italy," said Pista. "You, me, and Franchino."

Cecco put up his hand. "What?! Hold on, Pista. I don't know. It is a difficult trip." He looked down at the floor. "So much money. And fly in an airplane? I don't think those things are safe."

"Cecco, I am telling you, we go. Oenesta had a dream, so we have no choice. We are not getting any younger, and we will never see our home again if we do not go now."

Cecco sighed. Resistance was futile.

That same afternoon, Frank was sitting at his desk in Miss Florence Knodt's sixth-grade class when the telephone rang. Miss Knodt called him to her desk and said, "Frank, your parents are coming to pick you up. They have something important to tell you, so go out to the main gate and they'll meet you there."

At the gate Milma said, without preamble, "Get in the car. You are going to Italy with your grandparents and we don't have much time, so we're going to Hancock to get your passport photograph taken." What? Frank didn't know what to think, but it didn't matter, because the family had been given marching orders by Teopista.

A whirlwind of preparations ensued. Frank was told he would be gone for four months, including the first month of the next school year. Milma bought him new clothes that they crammed into two suitcases, and the travelers received vaccinations that made them all sick. The typhoid shot made Pista so ill that she almost cancelled the trip. She said she'd rather die.

Then Cecco got worried all over again about the cost. "Maybe it's too much to take Franchino," he said to Pista.

She had recovered by then. "You either buy three tickets or you buy one," she told him. "Either Frank comes with us or you go by yourself." Cecco drew from his hard-earned savings and bought three tickets.

The day of their departure, Teopista hosted the whole family for a huge meal, including her daughters and their families from Ohio. As dessert was served, she stood at the head of the table.

"Okay, it's time to clear the air," she said. "You people have been grumbling and griping and whispering ever since you found out we were taking Franchino on this trip. Well, I will tell you why he is going. It's because I like him better than any of the rest of you. Franchino is the one who pays attention to us. He shares meals, goes to the movies with me, writes my letters and addresses the envelopes, and ties my shoes. So I have learned to love him more. Some of the rest of you don't even live here. That's why I'm taking Frank to Italy." This speech by Teopista silenced the table. The aunts and uncles and cousins looked down at their plates and no one knew what to say.

The tension was relieved by the ringing telephone. It was the airport, calling to say that North Central Airlines would not be flying out of Houghton that day, so the first leg of their flight was cancelled. North Central hadn't missed a flight in months, but today was the day. Panic ensued. Pista, Cecco, and Frank had six bulging suitcases and had to make it to Chicago—more than 400 miles away—in time for their flight to New York.

One of Alimando's talents was to be good in an emergency. He found out there would be a flight from Iron Mountain to Chicago and offered to drive the travelers there. To make it on time, they had to leave immediately. Pista's daughters and their families hopped in their cars without a second glance, and sniffed as they set out for Ohio. Milma started to cry. When it dawned on Frank that he wouldn't see his mother for four months, he got a knot in his stomach. Milma gave him a bear hug, and said, "Frank, don't forget the journal I gave you. Write something every day so you will remember later. This will be the trip of a lifetime for you." He promised he would do this, and he did. The adventure had already started, with Pista's speech to the family.

It turned out there was no plane in Iron Mountain, so Allie drove them to Green Bay where they lucked into a plane at the gate. They rushed through the check-in, with Allie explaining to the agent that they were originally ticketed from Houghton to Chicago, but now needed to fly from Green Bay to Chicago instead. The three were let on the plane and it seemed all was well. However, that plane didn't go to Chicago. It landed in Milwaukee, with an announcement that this was the end of the route.

Cecco panicked. "Franchino, what are we going to do? You'd better go and ask." Cecco had been in America for forty years but did not speak much English, so he put his twelve-year-old grandson in charge. Frank went to the counter and said that they had to get to Chicago to make a connecting flight to New York.

"No problem," said the ticket agent. "You can take a train." They crammed their suitcases into a taxicab and drove to the Milwaukee train station, where they dragged the luggage onto a traincar and sat on top of the suitcases all the way to Chicago. This was not for a lack of seats on the train, but because Cecco was paranoid about someone stealing from them. This fear played an ongoing role in their travel saga.

After a time Frank could tell they were in the city, but had no idea where they were supposed to get off the train. It was night-time, which made it hard to see anything.

"Nonno, how far are we going to go on the train?"

Cecco scratched his head. "Well, when do *you* think we should get off?"

Again Frank was in charge. He saw that they were on the El, the elevated track, so he made a decision. "Nonno, we should get off here." They abruptly got off the train, and dragged their luggage down the steps to the street, which turned out to be nearly abandoned. They had no idea where they were. Now it was Frank's turn to panic. He saw a taxicab heading toward them, so he jumped out into the street waving his hands. "Taxi! Taxi!" He'd seen this in the movies, and it worked.

The taxi driver took them to Midway Airport. "What airline are you flying on?" he asked. Frank asked Nonno to give him the tickets, which were labeled "United." The driver dropped them off at the United terminal, and Cecco winced as he paid the fare. Inside the terminal, Frank found the United counter and presented the tickets.

"I'm sorry," said the agent, "but your flight left two hours ago."

Frank nearly started to cry. "What am I going to do? I have to get to New York with my grandparents because we're going to Italy."

The woman took pity on them. "Relax, young man. I can get you on an American Airlines flight." The trio hiked from United to American, and finally were on their way to New York. They landed at LaGuardia Airport, where Frank found an information desk. "Excuse me, where do we get our Alitalia flight to Italy?"

"Son, you're at the wrong airport," said the attendant.

"What?"

"You have to go to Idlewild International, across town."

"How do we get there?"

She explained that they could take a bus. Cecco reluctantly paid for three bus tickets, and in the early morning hours they arrived at Idlewild. The driver pushed their six suitcases out at the Alitalia terminal and they dragged them inside.

The ticketing area was completely deserted. "Franchino," said Cecco, "go find someone. Ma and I will sit here and watch the suitcases." Frank wandered around until he found an office, where he walked in and blurted, "I'm here with my grandparents and we're supposed to fly to Italy. What do we do?"

"Your flight isn't until tomorrow night," said a woman who

worked for Alitalia. "You're a day and a half early."

When Frank reported back to his grandparents, Cecco scratched his head. "Okay, we gotta wait. We will sit here."

Frank told the Alitalia woman what he'd said. "No," she responded. "You can't stay here all that time. Tell your grandfather you must go to a hotel and come back tomorrow afternoon."

"*Dio mio,*" said Cecco. "Okay, Franchino, you tell her we need a hotel no too 'spensie." Nothing expensive. A taxicab took them to her recommended hotel, with Cecco frowning at the meter the whole way. At the hotel, he told Frank to ask for the smallest possible room, with just one bed. "No too 'spensie." The hotel guy looked at them a little funny, but he offered a small room with a double bed and an easy chair. With the six suitcases crammed in, the floor was completely covered.

Cecco's plan was that they would sleep in shifts. Two people would sleep on the bed while the third sat in the chair and watched the luggage and Cecco's crotch. In a money belt under his pleated trousers he had his traveler's checks, plus $1,000 in cash that he had been given by South Range families to deliver to their relatives. He looked like he had a double hernia, but the money was as safe as humanly possible. Every two hours they rotated: two people sleeping on the bed, and the third watching the luggage and the crotch.

And so it transpired that Pista, Cecco, and Frank spent three days and three nights, subsisting on the very least amount of food and sleep they could stand, getting to Rome. On Cecco's instructions, they did not open their suitcases even once, so they arrived wearing the same clothes they'd left in. They were a stinking, exhausted, hungry trio when they got off the plane. And there were no relatives there to meet them.

"*Dio mio,*" said Cecco. "Now what?"

They decided to take a train to Lucca, which would require a 'spensie taxicab ride from the airport in Rome to the train station. Italian cabs are much smaller than American ones, so the travelers hunched on top of their suitcases for the twenty-mile ride. At the train station, they bought tickets—more grumbling about cost—and Frank asked Cecco if they could have sandwiches from a food cart. He was starving. In Italy, Cecco was the one who could communicate better, so he went over to the cart, returning with one salami sandwich and a bottle of wine.

"Nonno, one sandwich for all of us? And what about my Coca-Cola?" Frank was not happy.

"Is a big sandwich," he said. "We share. And the Coca-Cola was a whole dollar. This wine cost fifty cents." Frank and Pista had no choice but to split the salami sandwich three ways and wash it down with cheap Chianti. They perched on a hard marble slab at the train station and ate their first meal in Italy, preparing to wait nine hours for the train to Lucca.

Suddenly, a man came running into the station, yelling, "Rugani! Rugani!" It was Giuseppe's son Gino. He apologized for missing them at the airport, and enveloped them in a huge bear hug. All three dissolved into exhausted tears and finally, finally let family take them into their embrace.

Pista, Cecco, and Frank spent four full months in a tiny section of Tuscany, visiting their huge families. Frank had picked up a little Italian language from his grandparents, but in Italy people spoke so fast he couldn't keep up. He took to sitting with children in the piazza and pointing to objects around them. "In English this is 'table,'" he said. *"Tavola,"* they replied. The Italian kids liked to spend time with him because Milma had tucked a carton of Bazooka gum into his suitcase. He was followed around like the Pied Piper, and in exchange for a stick of gum he had Italian lessons any time he wanted. By the end of the visit, he was fluent.

In 1952, there were still some mountain villages near Lucca with no road access. The only way to get to Torcigliano Alto—site of so many memories for Cecco and Pista—was to walk up a steep hill. Pista was too large and unhealthy to walk, so the family arranged for an oxcart. On the cart they set a chair for Pista, surrounded by the six suitcases. It was quite a production to get her hoisted up there, which could have been awkward, but she was so delighted to be home with her family that the awkwardness rolled right off her back. She let out a huge belly-laugh, and the whole group laughed all the way up the hill.

Every reunion was emotional, but the greatest, by far, was between Francesco and his brother Giuseppe, who had not seen each other in forty years. They clung to each other, in tears, for a long time. Giuseppe then turned to Teopista and wrapped his arms around her girth. More sobbing. And then it was Frank's turn.

"Beppe, this is our grandson Franchino."

"Franchino, this is your Zio Beppe, your great-uncle."

"Franchino. Welcome to Italy. Welcome home." Zio Beppe drank in Frank with his eyes. The hug Frank received was from his blood grandfather, a truth Frank would not learn until many decades later. All he understood, in 1952, was that this family was as warm and loving as any he'd ever met.

As rich in spirit as the Ruganis were, they were materially very poor. Beppe had managed to buy some land, but his lifestyle was not much different from what it had been when he was *contadino,* a tenant farmer. His home had no running water or electricity. His wife, Oenesta, produced delicious meals on a charcoal-fired stove in the kitchen. The house always smelled like a blend of her gourmet cooking plus smoky charcoal. The family still made that charcoal from scratch, just as they had when Cecco and Pista were young. They still baked bread in an outdoor oven every day, and they raised small animals, including guinea pigs, for meat. Frank had trouble getting past his idea that guinea pigs were supposed to be pets. Sometimes he could not eat what was offered, and an accommodating relative would scramble an egg in olive oil, just for him.

One day Frank went out to fetch water with one of his cousins. The cousin asked what Frank wanted to be when he grew up.

"I want to be a priest," said Frank.

His cousin whipped his head around. "No, no! Don't even think about that! Do you know what happens when you become a priest?"

"What?"

"*Ti tagliano il ditto!*" This was not vocabulary Frank possessed, so he got his Nonno to translate it later. "They cut your thing off!" Frank's eyes opened wide. Cecco was pretty sure this was not true, but when he and Frank went to Mass at the local parish church, as they did every day, they found themselves glancing at the priest's robe. A seed of doubt about his second career choice began to grow in Frank's mind.

Cecco and Frank were the only two males at Mass during the week, but on Sundays everyone in the village was there. The men sat up front while the women knelt in the back. Cecco and Frank were teased afterwards because they were the only men with dust on their knees. The other men didn't bother to kneel for prayers.

After Sunday Mass, Oenesta served a breakfast of bread soaked in *caffe latte,* with extra milk and double sugar for Frank. After that tasty breakfast on their first Sunday, Beppe said to his brother, "Cecco, come upstairs. I have something to show you."

Before he left for America the second time, in 1912, Cecco had packed a trunk with the possessions he would not be taking with him. He figured he'd be back in a year or two, so he didn't give the process too much thought. By now, he'd forgotten the trunk even existed. But there it was, sitting in a corner of his old room.

"This is yours," Beppe said. "We have waited for you to come and open it."

Cecco took a breath and pried the trunk open. Inside were old clothing and some souvenirs. Then he found a very special item, a watch fob containing tiny photos of himself and Teopista when they were young. Pista's hand flew to her mouth when she saw it, and Cecco and Beppe exchanged a glance. It did not seem unusual to Frank that his grandparents' pictures would be together in a locket, but he did not know their story. All three had tears in their eyes, and Pista began to cry outright. Frank put his arms around her. "Ma, are you okay?"

"*Sì,* Franchino. *Va bene.* I am remembering things from long ago. Is okay. I am happy and sad, both." She kissed the top of his head.

Everywhere the travelers went in 1952, they saw evidence of the ravages of World War II. Cement walls were riddled with bullet holes, and piles of old tires and debris had not been cleared away. Beppe told Cecco that when the Nazis came through and ransacked people's homes, he and others hid out in the woods until it was safe to come out. The Germans took what little wine and food they could find, reducing the family to eating bark off the trees. Beppe had not been forthcoming in his letters during the war, but now he told the full, horrifying story.

Cecco had a lot of cash that people from South Range had given him to deliver to their relatives. To carry out this mission, he and Frank walked up and down hundreds of hills. The local people were poignantly grateful for a twenty-dollar bill. And they were desperate for news. Each family invited them in for wine and bread and to hear how their loved ones were doing in the Copper Country.

Everyone they visited drank wine, and half of everyone made their own. One day when Frank was staying with his Uncle Alipio in Picciorana, Alipio asked him to help dispense twenty gallons of home-fermented white wine into one-quart flasks, using a siphon hose. He showed Frank how to suck on the hose until he had a mouthful, and then to pinch the hose and aim it at the bottle. When the bottle was full, he had to pinch the hose again. Frank was clumsy with this process, so he ended up sucking on that hose quite a few times. When the job was done, he walked unsteadily back to the house with a goofy look on his face.

"Hi, Paolo!" he said to his cousin. "Isn't this a great day?" Paolo broke into hysterics. "You Americans can't handle your drink, eh?"

"What do you mean? I didn't drink." Frank had so little experience with alcohol that he didn't know he was inebriated. His Italian cousins had been drinking since they were toddlers. They made fun of their slurry American relative.

Nearly as emotional as the reunion between Cecco and Beppe was the meeting of Teopista and her sisters Corradina and Ersilia. Corradina was closest in age to Pista, the girl who as a teenager had strategized with Pista about how to manage the temperamental Faustino. Ersilia, the youngest, had been told repeatedly that it was Teopista who nursed her as an infant, when their mother was old and dry. Just seven years old when Pista left for America, Ersilia had pined for her return ever since. Dozens of letters between Pista and these sisters had crossed the Atlantic since 1912. Now they were together at last, drinking each other in and hugging and kissing non-stop.

One day Ersilia invited her nephew Frank to her upper-floor apartment in Lucca. "Franchino, we need some meat to dress up our marinara tonight. Watch this!" Lacking the money to buy meat, Ersilia practiced a local tradition. She put a row of dried corn kernels on a stick, and placed it partway out her porch window. She told Frank to sit quietly with her. Sure enough, a pigeon landed on the stick and began to eat the corn. The bird worked its way down the stick until he was inside the porch, at which point Ersilia pulled a cord to trap it behind a bamboo curtain. Frank watched, wide-eyed, as his great-aunt then caught the bird and wrung its neck.

"Ersilia, Nonno does something like this at home!" Frank was excited to tell her the story, using his newly acquired Italian. "We go up on the roof where Nonno has a rope and the inside of an old mattress – in English these are springs, I don't know the Italian word. He uses the rope to lift the springs a few feet above the roof. He puts dried corn underneath, and when blackbirds came to eat the corn, he lets go of the rope and the springs fall down on top of the birds. He kills the trapped birds with a shovel, and then we eat them. Well, I don't eat them because I don't like the bones."

Ersilia laughed and gave him a hug. "All good *contadini* know this trick, Franchino, and don't you forget it. You should eat that bird meat. Taste good!"

As the days passed in her childhood home, Teopista grew younger and funnier. Her peals of laughter made every conversation joyful. Tucked into her suitcase was a pair of black plastic glasses with a fake nose attached. At random times, she would put these on and pop into a room, or even walk down the street pretending nothing was out of the ordinary.

One morning, as the family dressed up to attend the first communion of a nephew, she stuffed some wool up the plastic nose to look like a mustache, and put the glasses on Frank. "Look, everyone, it's a miniature Uncle Beppe!" No one laughed harder than she did at her own joke. Another morning, Pista put on Cecco's pajamas and his hat, along with the glasses and nose, and snuck outside. She pounded on the front door, and when the children answered, they screamed that a beggar was at the house. She pulled off the hat and glasses and gave a huge belly laugh. "Fooled you!"

After the first communion service, the family went home for a celebration. To thank them for their hospitality, Pista had spent the entire previous day making a huge quantity of meat ravioli – a rarity for a poor family. Before the meal, her sister Elide said, "I think I'll just have a little glass of wine." She went in the kitchen and poured herself a huge glass, intending to gulp it down before returning to the party with a ladylike small portion.

"Aiiiieeeeeee!" They all heard screams from the kitchen. Elide was hopping around the room holding her throat. She had gulped white vinegar, thinking it was wine. Teopista laughed about this for days, tears running down her cheeks each time she re-told the story.

Pista and Cecco planned their trip to include *La Festa di Santa Croce,* the Feast of the Holy Cross in Lucca in mid-September.

Frank took a pass on pancakes made from lamb's blood—a local tradition—but he was transfixed by the luminary procession through the walled city. The glow of people's faces in the candlelight was magical. It was too bad about the problem of priests losing their *dittos,* he thought, because otherwise there would be nothing better than leading this solemn yet joyful procession.

Pista told Frank a story about the huge walnut crucifix inside the Church of San Martino. "Franchino, this crucifix was carved in the Holy Land and brought to Tuscany. There was an argument between Pisa and Lucca regarding where it should be kept. To settle the argument, they strapped the crucifix to the backs of a pair of oxen. 'Wherever the oxen take the crucifix,' they said, 'that's where we'll build a church in honor of Santa Croce.' The oxen ended up in Lucca, and that's why the cross is kept here." Frank stared at the massive symbol until his attention was diverted by his grandfather.

"Here, Franchino, I buy you a *bomboloni,*" said Cecco. "Better than any American doughnut, no?" Frank bit into the rich, fluffy, sugar-coated treat.

"Nonno, this is so good. I love Italy!"

Cecco beamed. He had a story for Frank, too. "Franchino, when I was a boy I walked all the way from Loppeglia to Lucca for this *festa,*" he said. "On the way down the hill everyone I met said, 'Cecco, bring me a whistle.' They wanted a clay whistle like the one we gave you today. 'Cecco, get me a whistle!' Everyone said it, over and over. Well at the bottom of the hill there was one guy with a different idea: 'Cecco,' he said, 'here are a couple of pennies so you can buy me a whistle.' You know what, Franchino?"

"What, Nonno?"

"That guy at the bottom was the only one who got a whistle from me. No money, no whistle! But the guy who asked nice and paid for his whistle, I made sure to get him one. Franchino, you treat people fairly, and they will treat you well in return. This I have learned."

As their four-month visit drew near its end, Corradina and

Ersilia took their beloved oldest sister aside. "Pista, we have something important to say to you."

"*Che cos'è?*" What is it? asked Pista. She braced herself for some kind of bad family news.

"It's just—Pista, don't go back to America! We want you to stay forever! It is so beautiful to have you here, and we can see how happy you are. The plan was always for you to return home one day, so do it now! Please?"

Teopista enveloped her sisters in a hug, as tears rolled down her cheeks. "Of course I am temped," she said. "This time has been happier than I could have imagined. But to move back here is different. I must think."

It was a perfect September day in Loppeglia. Pista wandered down old familiar village streets, breathing sweet air and day-dreaming of her childhood. Her parents were gone, but her dozen siblings had produced more than fifty children and a rapidly growing number of grandchildren. The embrace of her family was palpable. She and Cecco could live out the rest of their days right here. No more Copper Country winters, no more laboring in the grocery store, no more struggling with English, a language that had never come naturally to either of them.

"Cecco," she said when she returned from her walk, "come outside with me. It is a beautiful day." They sat on a bench and inhaled the air of home.

"*Caro,* we have something serious to discuss. Corradina and Ersilia came to me today with a proposal. They want us to move back home, to stay here for good." Cecco closed his eyes.

"This is what we thought from the beginning, remember? We would go to America only until we had enough money to come back and live better. It didn't work out right away, but we have that money now, our savings from the store. And we are much older, so we don't need as much as we did before. We could do it, Cecco. We could take Franchino home, pack up our things, and come back. We could live near your family in Torcigliano Alto, or here in Loppeglia. Either one would be beautiful. What do you think?" Pista was starting to get excited about the idea. Home!

Cecco looked at his wife. "*Sì*, the idea is tempting. But, Pista, what about our children and grandchildren? You want to leave them in America and maybe never see them again?"

Teopista exhaled. "Those daughters of ours in Ohio are no good and ungrateful. I don't care if I never see them again, seriously. Alimando and Franchino, well, yes, they matter. But we can write letters and they will come visit us. In exchange, Cecco, we'll have dozens and dozens of nieces and nephews and their children. There is family everywhere we look, here."

Cecco gazed out at the trees and was silent for a long time. "I don't know, Pista. Let's sleep on it. We will decide tomorrow."

Teopista tossed and turned all night. Usually so decisive, this time she was torn. Images of her life in South Range competed with the emotional reunions of this unforgettable trip. By morning she had nearly convinced herself to stay, to spend her last years in this place that had never left her heart.

Cecco didn't sleep much, either. By morning, he was ready to talk.

"Pista, I see how much you want this. It has been wonderful here, on this trip. Everyone speaks our language! The air smells so sweet and familiar. And our families have been so kind. But *cara*, I am not so sure it would be good for us to move back. Everyone here is so poor. I am too old for farm work, with my bad heart, so what would I do? I could not help them. And we have seen reminders of wartime suffering everywhere we look on this trip. This is not the same place we left, so long ago."

He paused. "Another thing, *cara*, is that we became Americans more than thirty years ago. We are Italian, yes, but maybe we are American even more."

It was Teopista's turn to be silent. After some minutes she nodded her head with a clarity Cecco knew very well. She had made up her mind. "You are right, Cecco. *Siamo Americani.* We are Americans. We go back to our family and our life in South Range."

She took a deep breath. "Okay, it's settled."

The next day, Pista spoke to her sisters in private. "I talked to

Cecco and we thought all night about what you said. My beloved sisters, here is the answer: I wish there were two of me—one to live here and the other in America. But there are not. I am an American now. Cecco, Franchino, and I are all Americans. We have a life there, and we will return there. But please do not be sad. You are I are closer now that we have seen each other during this perfect visit. We will write letters and say prayers for each other and be as close as sisters can be, with an ocean between us." Pista started to cry. "I love you so much, and I will miss you terribly, but this is what I must do." Now all three of them were crying.

"We knew this would be your choice, Pista," said Corradina. "We just had to ask."

A week later, the three travelers boarded their airplane home, after a torrent of tears between Teopista and her sisters at the airport. As they bucked their seatbelts, Teopista had one more message to deliver. She looked Frank straight in the eye and said, "Franchino, listen to me. We paid for you to come on this trip, but it was not free for you. You must stay in contact with your Italian family for the rest of your life. Do not let these connections get lost. I know you will do this, because you are the most responsible person in the family. Do not fail. This is *molto importante.*"

Frank was only twelve, but he understood the depth of his grandmother's request. He held her gaze. "Yes, Ma, I will do this. The Ruganis and the Marchis are my family, too. I will not forget them."

"Good boy," said Pista. "And now it's time to look forward, not back." That was the end of her tears.

Epilogue

Teopista Rugani lived for seven years after that trip to Italy. She lived to see her grandson Frank start college at the University of Michigan, the first in the family to go to college. She thought his dormitory building looked like a prison and the food was terrible, but she was deeply proud of his accomplishments. "Finally, we have achieved success in America," she said.

"But Franchino, listen carefully to what I tell you. You can see that I am ill. I will not live much longer, and I want you to have this ring I bought on our trip to Italy in 1952."

"No, Ma, don't talk like this!"

"Yes, Franchino, it is true and you must listen. After I die this family will break apart. There will never be peace between my children, and Pa isn't strong enough to hold them together. Your aunts are going to take everything. They won't leave you as much as a pair of torn silk stockings to remember me by. What I want you to do, when the time comes, is to go show your aunts this ring and tell them what I said about them. They do not deserve a moment of peace."

Teopista knew her time was short, but she was tormented by one other big unresolved issue. Because she had never located her first husband, Faustino Pini, she had never been able to divorce or annul their marriage. She had lived for more than forty years as a bigamist in the eyes of the church, and she would not go to heaven. She fretted about this incessantly.

Alimando stepped up. He enlisted a connected friend of his to conduct a nationwide search for Pini, and the search was successful. Pini was living with another wife, also in sin, in California.

"We will go there," said Teopista.

"Ma, are you strong enough to travel? It's a long way."

"For this, I would do anything," she said. "Father Cappo said he would be driving out there soon, to visit his uncle. We ask him to take us."

Father Cappo was a generous man. He agreed to add Pista and Cecco to the car, which already contained his parents, and to add a stop in central California, not close to San Diego where the Cappos were headed. More than 2,000 miles later, the group of five pulled up in front of a small house that matched the address Allie had unearthed. A woman was working in the garden.

"The rest of you wait in the car," said Pista. "This is my business."

"Are you Mrs. Pini?" she asked the woman.

"Yes," said the gardener quizzically. "Why?"

"So am I," said Pista. "Your husband is a bigamist."

"What?"

"Is he inside the house?"

The woman nodded. "I'll take you."

"No, I speak to him alone. Please stay out here with your flowers."

Teopista strode up to the front door and walked into the house. Pini was at a cluttered kitchen table eating lunch.

"Remember me, you captain of the whoremasters?"

Pini dropped his sandwich. "Teopista!"

"That's right, you worm." She looked him straight in the eye. "I have brought a priest here as my witness. After today I will never see you again and I hope you rot in hell." She walked out and let the door bang behind her. Pini choked on his pastrami.

Father Cappo took Teopista aside. "When we get back home, I will speak to the bishop on your behalf, Pista. Let's see what we can work out."

In the end, the priest and the bishop proposed a solution: If Teopista would renounce her forty-two-year marriage to Francesco, she could receive the sacraments and die in peace. This was a simpler path than obtaining a divorce for a marriage conducted fifty years before in Italy, for which Pista had no paperwork.

Pista and Cecco conferred. "This will not change anything between us, *caro*," she said. "We will still be married in our hearts, as we have been all these years. But we will be right with the church. I don't have much time left. God is waiting for me." Cecco agreed, with tears in his eyes, and gave her a tender kiss.

When the renunciation papers came through, Teopista rejoiced. She accepted the sacrament, sank back on her pillow, and transported herself to the Tuscan hills of her childhood.

Her wake lasted two full days, as the entire three-village area of South Range, Baltic, and Trimountain came to pay respects. Flowers overflowed the funeral home and a line snaked all the way around the block. Teopista had been loved, admired, and feared by everyone who knew her.

At the cemetery, Alimando's eyes were full as he tossed a fistful of soil onto the casket. "Goodbye, Ma. Now you can be with Beppino again."

Milma placed a flower on the coffin. "We didn't always see eye to eye, Teopista, but I grew to love you. Thank you for accepting me into your family, and caring for us all."

Frank openly sobbed. "Ma, what will I do without you? No one has been there for me the way you have. I will make you proud, I promise." He couldn't stop crying. Frank had gone through a phase of thinking he might like to run Rugani's Market for a living, but Alimando had ensured that his son learn how much thankless work the business required.

"Now that you've come to your senses," Allie had said after Frank had second thoughts, "I'm gonna give you three choices. You can be a doctor, a dentist, or a lawyer. We don't have any of these in our family yet, so you pick one." Frank didn't know what else to do, so he picked dentistry and began his coursework at the university. He would have loved to have his grandmother see him graduate, but it was not to be.

Francesco was beyond tears. "Pista, love of my life, if there is a heaven, I know it looks like Torcigliano Alto. Wait for me there in the orchard, okay? One day, I will join you. *Ti amerò per sempre.* I will always love you."

Alimando's sisters from Ohio approached the grave together. They wailed pitifully, and for so long that Frank couldn't take it.

"Give me a break, you didn't really love her!" he burst out.

"And you know what? Ma told me that after she died you would take everything. She said you would cheat us!"

"Frank!" Milma tried to take her son's arm but he yanked it away.

"I hate them!" he yelled, and ran from the cemetery.

"You ungrateful brat," said one of the sisters to Frank's retreating back. "She spoiled you rotten and all you did was grow into a rude, arrogant young man. You and your big shot college classes. I hope you fail!"

Milma buried her head in her hands.

And then the family gathered in the apartment above the store for a reception. Arguments were set aside, though not forgotten, and glasses raised repeatedly. "To Ma."

"To Ma!"

Riposa in pace. Rest in peace.